"I wasn't doing anything that you didn't want,"

Chance said, his voice low and rough.

Lucinda's head whipped around to him. "Well, I won't want it again! I may not have much in this world, Chance Delacroix, but I do have my pride and my independence. I won't let you take those away. Not you or any man!"

"Lucy, you're crazy if you think—"

"Yes, I'm crazy all right…damn crazy for thinking you might be different."

"Different from who?"

She looked at him, opened her mouth to answer, then closed it. She wasn't going to argue with him. She wasn't going to look at him, and most of all, she wasn't going to want him.

Dear Reader,

Where's the best place to find love this holiday season? UNDER THE MISTLETOE! This month, Silhouette Romance brings you a special collection of stories filled with spirited romance and holiday cheer.

'Tis the season for Christmas wishes, and nine-year-old Danny Morgan has a tall order. He wants to reunite his divorced parents. Will FABULOUS FATHER Luke Morgan be able to win ex-wife Sherri Morgan's love— and fulfill his son's dreams? Find out in Carla Cassidy's heartwarming romance, *Anything for Danny*.

Helen R. Myers brings us a wonderful romance about the power of true love. *To Wed at Christmas* is David Shepherd and Harmony Martin's wish—though their feuding families struggle to keep them apart.

Linda Varner continues the trilogy, MR. RIGHT, INC. with *Believing in Miracles*. Falling in love again may be out of the question for single dad Andy Fulbright. But when he meets Honey Truman, *marriage* isn't....

Look for more love and cheer with a charming book from Toni Collins. *Miss Scrooge* may not have much Christmas spirit, but it's nothing that a holiday with sexy Gabe Wheeler can't cure. Lucinda Lambert is running from danger when she finds protection and love in the arms of *A Cowboy for Christmas*. Look for this emotional romance by Stella Bagwell. And Lynn Bulock rounds out the month with the delightful *Surprise Package*.

Wishing you a happy holiday and wonderful New Year!

Anne Canadeo
Senior Editor

Please address questions and book requests to:
Silhouette Reader Service
U.S.: 3010 Walden Ave., P.O. Box 1325, Buffalo, NY 14269
Canadian: P.O. Box 609, Fort Erie, Ont. L2A 5X3

A COWBOY FOR CHRISTMAS

Stella Bagwell

Silhouette
R O M A N C E™
Published by Silhouette Books
America's Publisher of Contemporary Romance

To my editor, Mary Theresa Hussey,
for her patience, guidance and friendship

 SILHOUETTE BOOKS

ISBN 0-373-19052-2

A COWBOY FOR CHRISTMAS

Copyright © 1994 by Stella Bagwell

This edition published by arrangement with Harlequin Enterprises B.V.

® and TM are trademarks of Harlequin Enterprises B.V., used under license. Trademarks indicated with ® are registered in the United States Patent and Trademark Office, the Canadian Trade Marks Office and in other countries.

Printed in U.S.A.

Books by Stella Bagwell

Silhouette Romance

Golden Glory #469
Moonlight Bandit #485
A Mist on the Mountain #510
Madeleine's Song #543
The Outsider #560
The New Kid in Town #587
Cactus Rose #621
Hillbilly Heart #634
Teach Me #657
The White Night #674
No Horsing Around #699
That Southern Touch #723
Gentle as a Lamb #748
A Practical Man #789
Precious Pretender #812
Done to Perfection #836
Rodeo Rider #878
*Their First Thanksgiving #903
*The Best Christmas Ever #909
*New Year's Baby #915
Hero in Disguise #954
Corporate Cowgirl #991
Daniel's Daddy #1020
A Cowboy for Christmas #1052

* Heartland Holidays Trilogy

STELLA BAGWELL

lives with her husband and teenage son in southeastern Oklahoma, where she says the weather is extreme and the people friendly. When she isn't writing romances, she enjoys horse racing and touring the countryside on a motorcycle.

Stella is very proud to know that she can give joy to others through her books. And now, thanks to the Oklahoma Library for the Blind in Oklahoma City, she is able to reach an even bigger audience. The library has transcribed her novels onto cassette tapes so that blind people across the state can also enjoy them.

This is a pie I always prepare for my family at Christmas. And I promise no real cowboy can resist!

STRAWBERRY CRACKER PIE

3 egg whites
1 cup sugar
16 small square saltine crackers, crushed
$1/4$ tsp baking powder
$1/2$ cup nuts (I use pecans)
1 tsp vanilla
1 pint strawberries (crush into large pieces and sugar to your liking, or you may use frozen, already sweetened, berries)
whipped cream

Preheat oven to 350° F.

Beat the egg whites until stiff. Add 1 cup sugar slowly, the crushed crackers, baking powder, nuts and vanilla. Pour into buttered pie pan. Bake at 350° F until lightly browned, usually about 15 min. Cool. This will serve as the crust.

Spread fruit over crust, then cover all with whipped cream. Chill and serve.

Merry Christmas!

Stella Bagwell

Prologue

Lucinda Lambert stared cautiously at the brightly wrapped package on her coffee table. It was long and slender in shape, the paper printed with Santa Clauses and reindeer. She'd found it on the back steps of her apartment when she'd arrived home from work. That was enough to alarm her. No one had access to the inner courtyard of her apartment building, except the other tenants. Could she be that lucky? Was it possible the gift had merely come from a neighbor?

Seeing no other way of finding out, Lucinda reached for the small card that was slipped beneath the red ribbon. Her fingers shook as she opened the envelope, then everything inside her went cold and still as she read, "Merry Christmas, my darling Lucinda. All my love, Richard."

Fear clutched her heart, drained the blood from her face and left her hands clammy. It had been almost a week since her telephone had rung in the middle of the night, or an unmarked police car had followed her home from work. The

small reprieve had led her to hope this horrible nightmare
was going to end, that Richard was finally going to come to
his senses and realize she was never going to love him, much
less marry him.

Lucinda could see now that she'd been crazy to hope.
Christmas was little more than a week away, but obviously
Richard wasn't going to use the holidays to spread cheer and
goodwill. No, she thought sickly as she glanced once again
at the wrapped package, he was going to use Christmas to
spread his own special brand of evilness.

As if on cue, the telephone rang. Lucinda stared at it a
moment, then with a small groan hurried across the room
to pick up the receiver.

Perhaps it was Molly. She'd left her friend working late
tonight at The Fashion Plate. There was a chance she might
be having problems with the mohair cape she'd been sew-
ing.

"Hello," Lucinda answered warily.

"Hello, sweetheart. Did you get my Christmas package?"

The mocking masculine voice sent shivers of pure terror
along her spine. Without saying a word, she slammed down
the receiver and backed several feet away from the telephone.

Before she could reach the kitchen, it began to ring again.
Lucinda did her best to ignore the demanding sound and
tried not to think of the caller, who might be far across
town, or perhaps just across the street from her.

The doors and windows are locked, Lucinda. He can't get
to you, she fiercely told herself. But deep down, she couldn't
make herself believe that she was truly safe. If, or *when*
Richard finally decided to get to her, he could easily do it.
Being on the Chicago police force had taught him all the ins
and outs. It had also left Lucinda without any protection at

all. No one believed she needed to be protected from one of their finest homicide detectives.

Finally the incessant ringing stopped. But by then, Lucinda was shaking all over. She was also furious. She was sick of being afraid. She was tired of constantly looking over her shoulder and dreading the ring of the telephone.

Chicago was the only place she'd ever lived. But it wasn't a home to her anymore. It was a cage of fear and would be as long as Richard continued to harass her.

Squaring her slender shoulders and lifting her chin, she walked to the bedroom and pulled several suitcases out of the closet.

It was time she found a real home.

Chapter One

Lucinda leaned over the steering wheel and squinted through the small circle she'd just swiped upon the windshield. The misty rain that had been falling for the past fifty miles had turned into snow. Not just a few fat flakes drifting along in the wind; this stuff was coming down by the bucketfuls, turning the night into a white blur and making it impossible for her to see more than a few feet in front of the car.

For the past fifteen minutes she'd been straining her ears to catch a weather report on the radio. So far the only thing she'd managed to pick up from an Amarillo station was a cowboy humorist telling a story about a bull and a greenhorn rancher. And now, thanks to the fading radio station, she'd even missed the end of that, drat it!

The windshield fogged over once again and Lucinda flipped the defroster on high. It was the middle of December. She'd expected Texas to be cool, but a blizzard? Not in her wildest dreams. This was a southern state! At least it was far south of Chicago!

Lucinda supposed she should have stayed at Amarillo and gotten a room for the night. But ever since she'd crossed the line from Oklahoma into Texas, she'd felt the urge to press on. California was still more than a thousand miles away. The longer she could stay on the highway, the sooner she could get there.

But Lucinda hadn't planned on driving straight into this foul weather. Now she was going to be lucky if she made it to a town large enough to have a motel or a place of lodging. If she made it to a town at all!

"You've lost your mind, Lucy. Moving to California isn't going to make your life all sun and roses," her friend Molly had told her the minute she'd heard Lucinda was leaving. "Richard can always follow you out there."

"He won't follow me all the way out to California," Lucinda had protested. "Surely he's not that obsessed."

Molly glumly shook her head. "I'm beginning to think the man is crazy. He might do anything."

"That's why I'm leaving and you're not to tell anybody where I'm going."

"If you'd let the police—" Molly began only to have Lucinda interrupt her with a mocking snort.

"Do you hear yourself, Molly? Richard *is* the police."

Maybe her friend Molly had been right, Lucinda thought as she fiercely gripped the steering wheel. Richard could possibly follow her. But she had to take that chance. She had to find a new life for herself. Whether it was in San Diego or Los Angeles, she didn't know yet. She only knew that she was finally putting Richard and the hellish months of his abusive threats behind her.

"—snow and sleet with high winds and dangerously low temperatures. This winter storm—"

Apparently the weather was playing havoc with the antenna on her car. The man's voice faded into nothing. Lucinda desperately twisted the tuning knob, but it didn't help.

Oh well, she thought wearily, from the dim view she had before her, she didn't need a meteorologist to tell her it was bad out there. The wind had picked up considerably, slashing snow straight into her little car. The tall, yellow grass on either side of the highway was bent flat under the merciless gale, making Lucinda wonder how soon it might be before her car was blown off the road or into the path of a passing vehicle.

Perhaps she'd be better off if she stopped the car and waited for the storm to abate. But where? From the sketchy glimpses she could catch outside the windshield, there was no place to stop. This was a rural area she was traveling through, much of it open farm and ranching country. The four-lane highway had ended several miles back, leaving her on a narrow highway with hardly any shoulder.

"Damn!"

She shrieked the word as suddenly a loud pop exploded at the front of the car. The steering wheel jerked violently against her hands. Instinctively Lucinda reacted by stomping hard on the brake pedal, jamming it nearly to the floor. In response, the wheels locked and sent the car skidding sideways on the ice-slick road.

Frantically Lucinda jerked on the steering wheel to right the car back on a straight course. But it was too little too late. She was going to crash and there was nothing she could do about it.

"What the hell?" Chance Delacroix muttered as he topped a rise in the road and saw a small red car buried nose first in the ditch.

Quickly he eased the pickup off to the side of the highway and dug a flashlight out from under the seat. More than likely the car was empty, left by the owner until the weather cleared. But Chance couldn't, in all good conscience, pass it by without checking first. If someone was still in the car, it would only be a matter of minutes before hypothermia set in.

The moment he stepped out of the shelter of his warm pickup, bits of ice and snow smacked him straight in the face. Cursing, Chance tugged the brim of his cowboy hat lower onto his forehead and hurried across the wide ditch to the wrecked car.

It had Illinois plates and the back seat was piled high with bags and suitcases, but more important, a head of dark hair was pressed against the driver's window.

He rapped his knuckles against the window. "Hey in there! Can you hear me?"

There was no response. Or at least Chance couldn't hear any over the sound of the driving wind.

Gently, in case the driver was unconscious and not belted in, Chance opened the door.

Lucinda immediately felt something wet against her face and for a moment she thought she'd been dreaming and had woken up crying. But then a hand touched her forehead. A big, callused hand that smelled like man and snow.

Slowly she opened her eyes and found herself looking into a darkly shadowed face.

"Who—what happened?" she asked fuzzily.

"Looks like you met up with a patch of ice. Are you hurt?"

The voice was deeply masculine, very Texan and oddly soothing. She took a deep breath and tried to pull her senses together.

"I don't know." Frowning, she touched her fingers to her forehead as her eyes swept frantically around the dark interior of the car. "There was a loud pop and then—did I—" her gaze swung back to the stranger's shadowed face "—did I hit something?"

"I don't see anything else around here, lady, but you and a ditch."

Lucinda groaned as her wits gathered and reality began to settle in. "Is the car ruined?" She fumbled with the seat belt while inwardly cursing the fact that the interior lights had obviously gone awry.

Chance hadn't spared an extra moment to pull on his coat. Now he was getting wetter and colder by the second. Didn't this woman realize they were out in a blizzard? he wondered irritably.

"You can worry about the car later, ma'am," he said, raising his voice above the wind. "Are you all right?"

The belt finally snapped free. She pushed it out of the way. "I'm fine—I think. Except for my right foot. It feels like I must have twisted it, or banged it against something."

"My truck is just a few yards away. I'll take you to a doctor."

"Oh, do you think that's necessary?" She knew she was in a predicament, but that didn't necessarily mean she wanted to put herself into the hands of a total stranger. And she certainly didn't want to go to a hospital emergency room where they'd charge her several hundred dollars for five minutes of service. Money that she didn't have to spare.

She had a Midwestern accent, but Chance would have known she was a Northerner even without hearing her voice. She had that attitude about her that Texans like himself described as standoffish.

"Look, lady, you can't wait here for a tow truck! It could be hours before one is available. You'd freeze to death before then." He put one hand on her shoulder and another on her arm. "The D Bar D is only about four miles from here. We'll call a wrecker from there."

Lucinda grabbed her purse and coat from the passenger seat.

"The D Bar D?" she asked, darting him a frantic glance as he began to virtually lift her up and out of the seat, pulling her coat over her.

"My home."

Suddenly she was outside the car, cradled in his arms. Ice and snow pelted her face and the streaks of pain shooting through her ankle felt as angry as the freezing wind howling around them.

Even though Lucinda couldn't see her rescuer's face under the brim of his black Stetson, she could feel his chest and shoulders were wide and his arms strong as he began to carry her easily across the wide, soggy ditch to his vehicle.

Once he'd placed her on the bench seat and hurried around to the driver's side, Lucinda had collected herself somewhat. Pushing her dark hair behind her ears, she bent forward and tried to examine her foot.

"Do you think it's broken?" he asked gruffly.

The dome light came on and she jerked her head in his direction. "I hope not," she said through chattering teeth. "I don't think…" Her voice trailed off as she looked at him beneath the glow of the dome light.

That drawling, sexy voice had a face that was equally disarming. Crow black hair hung in wet curls around his angular features. Bits of ice and snow glistened on his tanned skin and spiked the thick sooty lashes that were now drooping over his gray eyes. Which, at the moment, were looking back at her, waiting for her answer.

Yet Lucinda couldn't get a word past her lips. All she could do was stare at him. Her eyes felt glued to his roughly hewn mouth, the long hawkish nose, the cocky jut of his jawline. Unable to suppress a shiver, she hugged her arms to her.

"I don't know. I've never had a broken bone. Have you?"

He took off his hat, quickly dusted the snow from the brim, then socked it back onto his head. "A couple. They hurt like hell."

He put the pickup into gear and carefully pulled back onto the highway. White sheets of snow slashed horizontally through the air, making visibility practically nil. Lucinda didn't know which was more threatening, the violent weather or this dark stranger who was taking her to God only knows where.

"Is this weather—isn't it unusual for Texas?"

Shaking his head with disbelief, he switched the wiper blades to a faster rhythm. "In case you hadn't noticed, Texas is big. What goes on down in the south is nothing like here in the Panhandle."

So he was telling her that blizzards were a normal happening around here. He must be thinking she was an idiot for driving in one.

"It was misting rain when I left Amarillo, I never thought I'd run into snow like this," she felt compelled to explain.

Chance didn't say anything, but he wanted to. It was damn stupid for a woman to be traveling alone at night. And in this weather! She had to be one of those flighty females who never thought before they acted.

"You must be in a hell of a hurry to get where you're going," he muttered. "Does your husband know you're out in this?"

The heater was running full blast but Lucinda felt cold in spite of the warm air rushing over her feet. "I'm not married."

Chance darted a quick glance at her. She wasn't married, so who or what was she trying to get to? A job? A lover?

"Well, I can tell you the highway on down to Roswell is a solid sheet of ice. In fact, parts of it are closed. But you would have never made it that far. You have to have a four-wheel-drive vehicle to travel on this stuff. Were you headed in that direction?"

Lucinda bit her lip. This man had just rescued her from a wrecked car in a freezing blizzard. She shouldn't mind his asking questions. But she was loath to tell him where she was going. She didn't want to leave any sort of trail behind her that Richard could follow.

Her eyes traveled over his dark face as she tried to decide whether he was a man to be trusted. "Yes. I'm working my way south to Interstate 10."

That didn't tell Chance much, but he didn't question her further. She looked frazzled, but then he supposed any woman who'd just slammed her car into the ditch would be a little distracted.

She was pretty though, Chance concluded, and young, too. He doubted she was a day past twenty-five. Straight brown hair spilled over her shoulders and down her back. Her eyes were also dark, but whether they were brown or green he couldn't tell.

At the moment he could feel those eyes studying him warily. "Well, miss, you haven't told me your name."

Lucinda looked away from him. She didn't want to tell him her name. That was too personal. And he didn't really need to know it, did he?

"You do have one, don't you?" he prompted when her silence continued.

Her eyes straight ahead, she nodded. "It's Lucinda Lambert. Lucy to my friends."

"Well, Lucy," he said as he carefully guided the pickup onto a graveled lane, "I'm Charles Delacroix. Most everyone calls me Chance."

From the corner of her eye, Lucinda noticed his snow-dampened shirt was white and obviously for dress wear. Gold-and-onyx cuff links glinted at his wrist while the toes of a pair of fancy black cowboy boots extended beneath the legs of his dark trousers.

He'd taken a chance on ruining his expensive clothing to rescue her from the wrecked car. That surprised her. All the men she knew would have stood back and waited for an emergency unit to arrive.

She let out a sigh. Maybe this man could be trusted. She prayed to God that he could be. "I've obviously interrupted your evening. Were you going to a party?"

"I was at a party. Until I went out for more lamb fries."

"Lamb fries?"

From the look on her face it was obvious to Chance that she didn't know what he was talking about.

"Yeah. They're, uh—a certain part of the bull that's considered a delicacy. Sarah Jane just had to have them. It's her engagement party, you see. She doesn't realize there's a blizzard going on out here."

He motioned to a grocery sack sitting between them. "Once the guests finish these off, that's it. I say let 'em fill up on steak."

Some woman named Sarah Jane wanted lamb fries, something that had nothing to do with a lamb, so this handsome hunk with his molasses voice had braved a blizzard to go get them and had rescued another damsel in distress along the way. Were all Texas cowboys like this one? Or was Charles "Chance" Delacroix something special?

Chapter Two

The home Chance Delacroix called the D Bar D turned out to be a sprawling Spanish-style ranch house. Along the driveway leading up to it, a maze of vehicles were parked at every available angle. It looked as if some guests had just left and others were in the process of leaving.

Lucinda stared in awe as Chance brought the pickup to a stop behind a dark green Jaguar. She'd known, just by looking at his clothes and the luxurious pickup they were riding in, that he wasn't a poor man. But she hadn't expected him to live this well!

"Do you think you can walk? Or do I need to carry you into the house?"

She darted him an anxious glance. "Do I have to? Go in there, I mean?"

He frowned as she inclined her head toward the brightly lit house.

"Where the hell would you want to go? Other than the house, there's only barns and stables and they aren't much warmer than being outside."

Lucinda had driven well over a thousand miles in the past two days. She was bone weary and now her car was wrecked and her foot was throbbing. She wished he could see that she wasn't in any shape to walk into the middle of an engagement party.

Clutching her coat protectively against her, she said, "I—I'd really rather—could I just sit in the kitchen while you call a wrecker?"

Biting down on a curse, Chance started to point out that she was being ridiculous, but something on her face stopped him. There was a haunted, vulnerable look in her eyes that tugged at him in spite of the fact that he normally couldn't abide a helpless woman.

Without a word, he jerked the gearshift into reverse, pulled away from the Jaguar and started around a driveway that led to the back of the house.

Oh brother, now he thought she was being ungrateful, Lucinda thought with a silent groan, and that was the last impression she wanted to give him.

"I'm sorry. I know I'm being a bother. It's just that I'm not up to meeting a roomful of strangers."

Her apology made Chance feel like a heel, though he wasn't quite sure why.

"Hell, don't apologize," he said more gruffly than he intended. "It isn't your fault that a party is going on."

He killed the engine and Lucinda scooted to the edge of the seat.

"It isn't your fault that I ran into the ditch, either," she told him. "I don't know what I would have done if you hadn't stopped to help me."

By now the inside of her car would be ice-cold. Even if the motor had started, she wouldn't have been able to drive it out of the ditch. And trying to walk in the blizzard with an injured foot would have been asking for deep trouble.

The sobering thought sent a shiver of fear through her. She looked at him and tried her best to smile, though she could feel her lips trembling. "I'd be glad to pay you for all your trouble. But that sounds pretty pathetic, doesn't it, when we both know you probably saved my life?"

Chance frowned at her. She was making him out to be some sort of hero. And that made him very uncomfortable. The last thing Chance could ever be was a hero. Especially to a woman.

Turning away from her, he reached for the door handle. "Keep your money. You can repay me by staying off the roads in weather like this."

Before she could say more, he climbed out of the truck and came around to her side. Lucinda quickly opened the door and lowered her feet toward the snowy ground below.

"Wait," he said as she started to slide out of the truck. "You'd better let me carry you."

Lucinda didn't want him to carry her. She wasn't exactly sure why. She only knew that he was big and strong and male. The idea of being that close again to him left her feeling awkward and hot faced.

"I—I can probably walk," she quickly blurted, and slid the rest of the way to the ground before he had a chance to reach for her.

"Ooh!" The one word came out in a shocked gasp as her injured foot took her weight.

Cursing under his breath, Chance didn't wait for her permission; he swung her up into his arms and started toward the house.

"It always feels good to prove a point, doesn't it?" he asked mockingly.

Trying her best to ignore him, Lucinda gritted her teeth as the pain in her foot shot through her leg, then gradually began to subside.

"I know you're anxious to get back to your fiancée," she told him. "As soon as you get me inside to a telephone, I'll be all right and you can return to your party."

As Chance stepped upon the porch and walked along its length to his private entrance, with Lucinda still in his arms, it dawned on him that she believed he was celebrating his own engagement. Which didn't really matter, he supposed. He didn't know this woman and she'd be leaving as soon as a wrecker pulled her car from the ditch. Still, he didn't like her thinking he was engaged. He wasn't a marrying man and he made sure everyone knew that.

"Sorry, but you're wrong on two counts. I don't have a fiancée and a telephone isn't all you need."

He walked through a side door leading from the porch, fumbled for a light switch, then carried Lucinda inside. From her lofty perch in his arms, she could see they were in a bedroom. From the masculine look of the pine furniture and sparse decorations, she could only guess the room was his.

Knowing that only made her feel more awkward as he gently placed her down on the bed.

"Now," he said, taking a step back from her. "Stay right there and I'll go get the doctor."

Lucinda's heart gave an odd little thump inside her chest. He was looking at her as if he were almost pleased to see her lying on his bed. But that couldn't be. He didn't know her and it was hardly likely that he welcomed the intrusion she'd made on his evening.

"Did you say doctor?"

Before he could answer, she planted both hands on the mattress and vaulted to a sitting position. "Oh, please—I don't want you to go back out in this weather. It's too dangerous! Besides, I'll be fine. Really. I don't need a doctor."

She was practically pleading with him and Chance got the impression that she wasn't at all used to having anyone help or look after her. But that could hardly be right. She was a beautiful woman. She'd probably always had men at her beck and call.

Shaking his head at her, Chance put his hand on her shoulder and pressed her gently back down on the bed. "You let me decide what you need."

As Lucinda looked up at him, she was struck by how much larger he was than she'd first imagined. He had to be at least two or three inches over six feet and carrying two hundred pounds of pure muscle. Just looking at him sent a surge of adrenaline pouring through her, making her heart gallop beneath her breast. Not with fear. No. This man didn't scare her. He excited her in a way that made her feel warm and womanly and totally foolish.

"Do you always have a habit of ordering women around?" she couldn't help asking.

One corner of his mouth lifted as though he found her question amusing. "Only stubborn Northerners. The women around here know when to let a man take care of them."

Certain that all the oxygen must have left the room, Lucinda drew in a deep breath. "And you know how to do that? Take care of a woman?"

His eyebrows peaked as he slowly took in her long, disheveled hair, pale face and, finally, the shape of her legs encased in bright red leggings.

"I guess I should know. I've been doing it for years."

Lucinda didn't know exactly what he meant by that and she certainly wasn't going to ask him. Just having him look at her in such a possessive, male way was enough to stain her cheeks with bright red heat.

Chance could see that he'd embarrassed her and that surprised him. Modesty seemed to have gone out of style with most of the women he knew. Seeing the uncomfortable color on Lucinda Lambert's face made him wonder just what kind of life she'd led up until now.

"Don't worry, Lucy," he said, suddenly struck with a need to reassure her. "The D Bar D isn't a bad place to be stranded."

Before Lucinda could say anything to that, he went on out the door that led into the main part of the house. Which was probably a good thing. Getting personal with a man like Chance Delacroix would be inviting trouble. And she already had enough of that to deal with.

Sighing heavily, she looked around the large room. Surprisingly, most of the furniture was old. Since it was all in excellent condition, Lucinda knew it was very valued and had probably been handed down through family generations.

A denim shirt was tossed across the arm of a wooden rocker, and several toiletry items were scattered on the dresser top. Photos looked at her from different perches around the room, but Lucinda was too far away to see them clearly, though she suspected they were probably all family. Chance Delacroix seemed that sort of man. Even if he wasn't married or engaged.

Closing her eyes, she rubbed her hands over her face. Dear God, how had she ended up here in this strange house, in the bed of a man she didn't know? Her car was probably out of commission and from the way it felt, her foot, too. What was she going to do?

She'd barely had time to consider the question when Chance walked back through the door. A tall, gray-haired man followed closely behind him.

"Lucinda, this is Doc Campbell. He likes partying better than he does doctoring, but I talked him into looking at your foot."

"Hello, Doctor," she greeted, grateful for the kind smile on his face.

"Don't listen to this one," he told Lucinda, while jabbing his elbow back at Chance's rib cage. "If he's got his mouth open, he's lying. And I ought to know, 'cause I delivered him into this world."

Expecting him to look at her foot first, she was surprised when the doctor came and sat down on the side of the bed.

Taking her hand in his, he said, "Chance, if you'll be kind enough to go get my bag from my car, I'll check this pretty young woman over."

To Lucinda he said, "Don't worry your little head about a thing. You couldn't have picked a better place to mend than the D Bar D."

To mend? She had no intentions of staying here long enough to mend, and from the scowl on Chance's face, she knew he had no intentions of letting her.

"What's the matter with you?" Doc asked, glancing up at Chance, who was still standing a few steps away from them. "Are you waiting for the molasses to run? Get gone, boy."

Chance left the room and Lucinda was relieved to feel her heartbeat slow to a more normal pace. She didn't know what it was about the man, but he definitely unsettled her.

"Now tell me about this car accident," the doctor spoke up. "Chance mentioned that you were a little rattled when he found you."

Glad to put her mind on anything other than her dark rescuer, Lucinda nodded and proceeded to tell him what had happened up until the moment Chance had found her in the car.

She'd barely gotten the whole story out when the door leading from the porch opened and Chance entered the bedroom. Snow and sleet covered his clothes and the black bag he handed to the doctor.

The older man grabbed the medical bag and shook it in a way that reminded Lucinda of a dog ridding its coat of water. "You'd better get out of those clothes, Chance, or you'll be in bed here with Miss Lucinda."

"If that's the case, maybe I should leave them on," Chance said.

Lucinda's gaze whipped over to where Chance was hanging his snow-damp Stetson on a hat rack. There was a smile on his face. Or maybe it was closer to a mocking grin, she thought. Either way, it was the first one she'd seen on the man tonight.

If his words and the twist to his lips hadn't been so suggestive she would have let her eyes linger on the raw good looks of his face. But the idea of being in bed with him was such a provocative one, she had to lower her eyes back to the doctor and safer ground.

"Get out of here, Chance, and let me examine my patient," Doc told him. "And when you get done changing your clothes, bring us back some brandy. I expect this young woman could use a bit of warming."

Chance winked at Lucinda. "Doc, you're gonna give Lucy the wrong impression. She'll be thinking you're the boss around here instead of me."

Lucinda couldn't remember when a man had ever winked at her. Was he actually flirting? Or had he simply been trying to tell her that Dr. Campbell was a longtime friend and that's why he put up with the old man's orders? Whatever the reason, that wink had left Lucinda feeling strangely hot and bothered.

Dr. Campbell chuckled softly. "Maybe if your mama would marry me I'd help you do a little bit of bossin' around here. But as it is, I guess you're the only top dog on the D Bar D."

Crossing to a closet, Chance pulled out a pair of jeans and a red shirt. "I wouldn't worry, Doc. Mama will come around to marrying you one of these days," he said, then added as he started out the door, "I'll bring that brandy back in a few minutes."

Once Chance was totally out of sight, Lucinda exhaled an unconscious sigh and closed her eyes. That man had about as much presence as the winter blizzard wailing out there over the plains. And she was stupid for letting it affect her.

Dr. Campbell pulled out a stethoscope and a blood pressure cuff. While he wrapped it around her upper arm, he glanced at her swollen ankle. "I know you're more worried about your foot than anything. I'll get to that in a minute."

Lucinda tried to relax as he pumped up the cuff and listened to the fold of her arm. After a moment, he gave a satisfied grunt. "Just a little elevated, but I'll blame that on Chance. He seems to do that to all the women."

"He's—certainly not like any of the men I knew back in Chicago."

The doctor laughed. "No, I expect not." Flashing a pin light in her eyes, he continued to talk. "Chance isn't always easy to read. But he's a good man. I used to be a bit like him myself. But thirty-five years does a lot to a man. I'll bet you wouldn't believe I was a favorite beau among all the young ladies in this county."

"I'm sure I could believe it," Lucinda said politely, while thinking she'd never had a doctor like this one. Even though he was obviously in his sixties he was still a handsome man. His clothes were expensive and tasteful and she knew in spite of his casual demeanor he was a very educated man.

"Is—Mr. Delacroix always this way?" she asked as the doctor put away his light.

With his palm, he pressed down on her abdomen. "What do you mean?"

Lucinda licked her lips. She shouldn't be asking the doctor anything about Chance Delacroix. But since she was now in the man's house, she didn't think a question or two was that out of place. "Well, I mean, does he go out of his way to help people? He could have driven on by me tonight."

"Like I said, Chance is a good man. He doesn't know it, but he is. His father was a generous man, too. God rest his soul." The doctor suddenly looked up at her. "You're not pregnant, are you?"

The question left her with an overwhelming sense of relief that things between her and Richard hadn't gotten that far. "No. There's no possibility of that. Why, is something wrong?"

He gave her a reassuring smile. "Nothing is wrong. I just wanted to make sure there wasn't a little one in there that had been shook up."

The doctor turned his attention to her foot. Lucinda winced with pain as he took it between his hands and flexed it first one way and then the other.

"You trying to break it more, Doc?"

Through the pain, Lucinda heard Chance's voice coming into the room. She opened her eyes to see he was carrying a tray holding a cut glass decanter, three matching glasses and a plate of food.

Lucinda had thought him attractive before in his dress shirt and trousers, but now in jeans and a red cotton shirt with its long sleeves rolled back against his forearms, he looked like a handsome devil. One that knew it perhaps, but would never think of flaunting it.

"I've been a doctor for nearly forty years, Chance. I think I know a little bit about what I'm doin'."

Chance placed the tray on a table beside the bed then stood by Lucinda's shoulder as the doctor finished his examination. While he'd been out of the room changing clothes and waiting for his mother to fix a plate of food, he'd kept telling himself that the little northern snowbird he'd found in the ditch wasn't really that pretty. She was just an ordinary young woman who didn't have enough common sense to stay off the highway during a blizzard. But now that Chance was close to her once again, he had to admit to himself that there was nothing ordinary about her.

The red mohair coat she'd hurriedly thrown around her shoulders was now tossed, along with her purse, to one side of the bed. The loosely knit sweater she was wearing came down to her thighs and was black. Buttons lined the front of the garment and all were fastened, except for the top three where the collar fell away from her throat. Her skin was ivory pale, making the red velvet ribbon she wore as a choker around her neck even brighter.

If Chance allowed his eyes to dip lower, he knew he would see the faint shadow between the slight swell of her breasts. But he didn't allow himself that pleasure. It had been a long time since he'd been interested in a woman, physically or otherwise. He certainly wasn't going to let a total stranger change his habits.

"I called the wrecker service," he told her. "It will probably be tomorrow afternoon before they can get your car to you."

Her dark eyes jerked up to his and Chance was taken aback by the desperation he saw in them.

"Tomorrow afternoon!" she gasped. "But that's—I have to be gone before then!"

Chance exchanged glances with Doc, who'd also noticed the frantic sound in her voice.

"Why?" Chance asked. "Do you have a family emergency?"

Lucinda was in an emergency all right. But it had nothing to do with family and everything to do with getting as far away from Chicago as she could possibly get.

"I don't have any family," she said.

Chance had long considered himself tough hided and he intended to stay that way. As far as he was concerned, getting sentimental and soppy made a person vulnerable. But hearing Lucinda say she had no family tore right into him. A beautiful little thing like her surely had folks out there somewhere who loved and looked after her.

"You don't have anyone you need to notify and let know you're safe?"

Lucinda shook her head, wondering what Chance would think if he knew she'd just severed all ties with the only home and friends she'd ever had.

"No," she told him. "I have a friend who's expecting to hear from me tomorrow or the next day. But that's all."

Dr. Campbell eased her foot back onto the bed and stood up. "Well, you're going to need to take it easy on that foot for the next few days. It isn't broken, but the tendons around your ankle have had a pretty nasty wrenching."

Now that she knew her foot wasn't actually broken, getting back on the road was her major concern. "How soon will I be able to drive?" she asked him.

"I wouldn't advise it for two or three days. Even then I certainly wouldn't drive for long hours. Keeping your foot in that same downward position will only cause it to swell and ache."

What little bit of hope Lucinda had been desperately trying to hold on to vanished with the doctor's warning. What
was she going to do now? The nearest town with a motel was
Hereford and that was probably a good twenty miles back
toward Amarillo. Even if she had her car and was able to
drive, the roads were probably already becoming impass-
able.

Dr. Campbell moved to the nightstand and poured a small
amount of brandy into one of the glasses. "Drink this," he
ordered, handing it to Lucinda. "And try to relax. In a few
minutes Chance can find you some good old-fashioned aspirin for your pain."

Lucinda thanked him, then took a careful sip of the
brandy.

Satisfied that his patient was going to follow his orders,
the doctor left the room. However, the moment he was out
of sight, Lucinda sat up and swung her legs over the side of
the bed.

"Where do you think you're going?"

The authoritative tone in his voice took her by surprise.
As Dr. Campbell had said, Chance might be the top dog
here on the D Bar D, but he definitely wasn't her boss. After the torment Richard had put her through, she wasn't
going to take any man's orders.

"I'm getting up. I've got to figure out how to get to a
motel." She took one last sip of the brandy, then placed the
glass on the nightstand. "Surely some of your guests will be
going home soon. Perhaps I could catch a ride with them to
the nearest town?"

His mouth compressed to a disapproving line. "Most of
the ones who live in town have already gone home. The rest
are ranchers who live even farther out. Besides, with weather
like this, I'm sure all the motel rooms around here are already filled."

And you should have thought about all of this earlier, his expression said. Well, maybe she should have known better than to keep driving after dark and straight into a snowstorm, Lucinda thought, but her predicament wasn't entirely her fault. She wasn't familiar with Texas or its violent weather.

"Then what do you suggest?" she asked.

Before he could answer, her face brightened with another thought. "Could *you* get my car out of the ditch? I'd pay you double what a wrecker service would charge."

That desperate sound was back in her voice again, and Chance could only wonder who or what was making her so frantic to leave his home.

Pulling a bottle of aspirin from a drawer on the nightstand, he shook three of them into her palm. "Here, take these and forget about your car. It wouldn't do you a bit of good tonight, anyway."

Clutching the aspirins tightly in her fist, Lucinda stared at him. "But I can't stay here!"

She'd barely spoken above a whisper and, if anything, her face had gone even whiter. Chance was beginning to wonder if she was one of those women prone to hysterics. If she was, then she'd come to the wrong place.

"Why not? The D Bar D isn't the Ritz, but it's comfortable. And we have plenty of room."

Lucinda couldn't remember one person back in Chicago being so generous to her. Nor could she think of anyone who would trust a total stranger to stay overnight in their home.

Chance could see that his invitation had overwhelmed her. Along with gratitude, there was a lost, wary look on her face that made Chance want to take her in his arms, smooth his hand over her long hair and assure her that she would be all right. It was an awkward feeling for him and one that he didn't welcome, but it was there just the same.

"But you don't know me," Lucinda pointed out. "I could be a dangerous person."

Chance figured Lucinda Lambert *was* dangerous. But not in the way she meant. The only thing around here she might be a threat to was his common sense. But he could hardly tell her that. No more than he could send her out in a blizzard to find her own way to Roswell, or wherever the hell she'd been headed for tonight.

One corner of his mouth cocked upward into a wry grin. "I'm a big guy. You don't scare me too much."

He was trying to ease her mind, and for the first time since he'd pulled her out of the car, she felt a little better. Surely Richard couldn't track her down tonight, and tomorrow afternoon she'd have her car back. By then the sun might even be out and the snow would begin to melt.

Lucinda had to look at things positively. More than anything she didn't want to fall apart in front of Chance Delacroix and have <u>him</u> thinking she was a totally helpless female.

Moistening her lips, she lifted her eyes back up to him and was immediately struck by how familiar he already seemed to her. No matter where she went in the future, or how much time passed, she had a feeling she would never forget this man's gray eyes or slow, sensual voice.

She cleared her throat, then said quietly, "Thank you for—helping me like this. I—"

Her words trailed away in awkward silence and Chance suddenly realized he didn't want her to be grateful, he wanted her to be happy.

"Don't think anything of it. Christmas is just a few days away," he said, "and I'm in a generous mood. If you want to thank me, take those aspirins and eat the food Mother fixed for you."

"I will," she promised, then smiled at him. A wide, generous smile that lighted her green eyes and dimpled her cheeks.

Chance didn't smile back. He was too struck by her beauty and the knowledge that he really didn't want to leave the room. He wanted to stay here, keep looking at her, talking to her. He wanted to know exactly where she'd come from and where she was going. Most of all, he wanted to know why she was alone and why he cared that she was.

"Good night, Lucinda."

"Good night."

Chapter Three

So what now, she asked herself after he'd closed the door behind him. Are you supposed to stay here in this room? In *his* bed? Even if it was nearly Christmas, she didn't think he intended to be that generous.

It finally dawned on her that she was still holding the aspirins Chance had given her. She swallowed them down with a sip of brandy, then reached for the plate of food on the nightstand. There were several finger sandwiches filled with an assortment of meat, crackers slathered with dip, several types of cheeses and a slice of chocolate cake.

She'd started one of the sandwiches when the door opened and a tall, auburn-haired woman stuck her head inside the room. "Do you feel like company?" she asked.

"Of course," Lucinda told her while thinking the woman could only be Chance's mother. Other than the color of their hair, the resemblance between the two was very strong.

"I'm Dee, Chance's mother. I'm sorry I haven't been in to see you earlier, but my daughter's engagement party was

going on and most of the guests decided to say their good-
byes about the time you and Chance got here."

It seemed incredible to Lucinda that this woman would
even think it necessary to apologize to her. "Oh, please—
don't think you need to treat me like a guest. I'm more of an
intrusion than anything."

"Don't be silly," Dee said with a smile. She took a seat on
the bed beside Lucinda. "Anyone who's a friend of my
son's could never be an intrusion."

"But we're not friends," Lucinda felt obliged to point
out. "I just met Chance when he stopped on the highway to
help me."

Laughing, Dee reached over and patted Lucinda's hand.
"Doc says you need to rest your foot for a few days. By then
you'll be a friend to the whole family."

It was on the tip of Lucinda's tongue to tell Chance's
mother she had no intention of staying on this ranch for a
few days, but she kept the words to herself. Dee Delacroix
was being warm and gracious, and right now Lucinda
thought it best to simply accept her hospitality.

"I told your son I didn't want to be a bother."

A smile still on her face, Dee shook her head. "And you
won't be. What with getting ready for my daughter's wedding in May and Christmas and having you as a house-
guest, well, this is going to be an exciting place for a change.
I love it," she said happily.

Yes, but would Chance? was all Lucinda could think
about.

"Now," she said, rising to her feet. "I'll go get you some
things of Sarah Jane's so you can change and be more
comfortable. There's a private bathroom right through that
door." She pointed to Lucinda's right. "And while you're
changing, I'll start getting the spare bedroom ready for you.
Is there anything special you need in the meantime?"

At the moment, Lucinda felt so bewildered by all that had taken place this evening she could hardly think, period. "No, thank you. I'm fine."

Out in the kitchen, Chance poured himself a cup of coffee and carried it over to the breakfast counter. The entire room was a mess. Dirty plates, glasses, cups and partially emptied containers of food took up every available inch of counter space, besides filling the sink and covering the top of the cookstove.

Chance cleared a spot for his elbow, then straddled one of the bar stools. He was just lifting the cup to his lips when his mother came into the room carrying a tray loaded with party leftovers.

"There you are," she said brightly. "I hadn't seen you in the past few minutes. I thought you might have already gone to bed."

He couldn't go to bed. Or at least not his own bed. The Chicago snowbird was in it. He'd have to carry her to her own room first. "Not yet. I thought I was hungry, but after seeing this mess I've changed my mind."

Dee emptied the tray into a garbage pail. "There's some chocolate cake left around here somewhere."

"What about the lamb fries?"

Dee laughed. "They ate them as fast as I could fry them. Not a crumb left."

Chance frowned. "Well, it was sweet of Sarah Jane to remember and save some for me. I guess it slipped her mind that *I* was the one who braved a blizzard to go get them for her."

Still chuckling, Dee began to fill the double sink with warm water. "A lot of things slip Sarah Jane's mind here lately. But that happens to a person when they're in love and about to get married. Or have you forgotten?"

Chance grimaced. It wasn't like his mother to bring up Jolene. She knew it brought back painful memories to him. "I've made a point to forget, Mother."

Dee looked over at her son. "You know, I used to think you were right. That you should try to forget everything that happened with you and Jolene. But after your father died I learned that trying to block out memories just doesn't work."

He didn't say anything. Dee squirted liquid soap into the water, then tossed in a sponge. After a moment she said, "You know, it was a good thing Sarah Jane begged you to go to the grocery store. Otherwise, that young lady would have more than likely froze to death."

"I wouldn't go so far as to say that. Someone else would have probably stopped to help, eventually," he told his mother. But to be honest, each time Chance thought of Lucinda being stranded in such dangerous weather, it sent a shiver down his spine. He did thank God that he had stopped to look in her car.

"Someone else didn't. You did." She picked up a scouring pad and scratched at the skillet. "She sure is a pretty little thing."

"There's pretty women around here, too, Mother," Chance pointed out.

"That's true. But Lucinda is one of those with true beauty. She doesn't need to paint it on." She glanced at her son. "Did she tell you much about herself?"

Feeling edgy and restless, thinking about carrying Lucinda from his bed and into another, Chance left the bar stool and carried his coffee over to a plate glass door that looked out onto the back porch. "Not really. Just that she was headed south. And she seemed to be in an all-fired hurry to do that."

"Hmm. Well, she's probably anxious to join her family for Christmas. It's so lonesome to be away from your loved ones at this time of the year."

Chance stared at the thick, blowing snow, but in it he was seeing Lucinda's face when she'd confessed that she had no family. "She doesn't have any family. She did say that much."

"You don't mean it?"

Chance nodded grimly at his mother's shocked question. "That's what she said, and I can't think of why she would lie about such a thing. But then people are strange these days. She might be on the run from the law or something and just doesn't want anyone to know where she is."

Her dish washing momentarily forgotten, Dee frowned at her son. "You'd never make me believe that. She's as innocent as a lamb. I can see it in her eyes."

"You think everyone is good," Chance told her.

"They are. I made a point of taking you to Sunday school year after year just so you would know that."

Chance didn't bother asking his mother if she thought rapists and murderers were good, too. She'd merely remind him that all human beings had to have some redeeming qualities hidden away in them.

"You're too trusting, Mother. It's a good thing we don't live in a high-crime area. You'd be in trouble before you turned around."

Dee made a clucking noise with her tongue. "Chance, you've gotten so cynical. Your daddy would hate that if he knew it."

Stan Delacroix had died ten years ago. Chance had just turned twenty-one at the time. And though he hadn't been emotionally ready to take on the responsibilities of running the D Bar D, he'd made himself rise to the task. His mother and sister had looked up to him, depended on him to make sure their home and financial security would always be there for them.

It had been a big task for a young man who'd already had his hopes and dreams shattered with the loss of his young wife and child. If Chance was cynical, as his mother had said, then he felt he had a right to be.

"I'm not cynical, Mother, just realistic." Turning away from the glass door, he placed his cup with a pile of dirty dishes on the end of the cabinet counter. "By the way, where's Sarah Jane? Isn't she going to help you with this mess?"

"I sent Sarah Jane to bed after she helped me get the spare room set for Lucinda. She was tired."

Chance groaned. "You spoil that girl rotten. It wouldn't hurt her to do a little work around here."

"She worked like a dog getting things ready for this party tonight. Besides, she'll be gone in a few months and I won't get to spoil her anymore," Dee said wistfully.

"Well, don't stay up too long." Chance leaned over and kissed his mother's cheek. "I'm going on to bed. Feeding tomorrow is going to be hell. I just hope I don't find any dead calves."

Dee patted his shoulder. "You worry too much, son."

It was his job to worry, his responsibility to see that the ranch and his family remained intact. And sometimes the load made him feel very old.

"Chance?" Dee twisted her head around to her son as he started out of the room. "Do you think the highway will be passable tomorrow?"

"Maybe in a Jeep, but not for regular car travel. Why? Did you need something from town?"

"No. I was just wondering about your new friend's car. I'd like her to stay a few days. It would be nice to have a fresh face around here at Christmastime."

Fighting the urge to smile, Chance rubbed his hand over his chin and jaws. His mother would never change. She was hopelessly lost with a checkbook, she never remembered dates or appointments, and after thirty-some years on the ranch she still wouldn't climb onto a horse, but she loved people and if she could manipulate them to her way of thinking she'd go at it gung ho. In spite of all that, Chance wouldn't change a thing about Dee. He loved her just as she was.

"She's not my new friend, Mother. And as for her staying, I wouldn't put any stock in it. She's got all the markings of someone on the move. As soon as the highway clears, you can bet she'll be gone."

Dee pushed absently at the curls across her forehead. "Oh well, maybe we can change her mind about that. You will try, won't you?"

It had been a long time since he'd spent more than a few minutes with a woman who wasn't kin to him. He'd almost forgotten what that felt like. Until tonight when he'd brought Lucinda home with him.

Maybe it would be nice to have Lucinda Lambert's company for a few days, he thought. She'd definitely be a treat for his eyes. And as for him being tempted to flirt with her? Well, what would it hurt if he did? He was a man, after all, and it wasn't as if he were going to do anything foolish like fall in love with the woman.

"I'll see what I can do," he told his mother.

When Lucinda woke the next morning the bedroom was cast in a gray, eerie light. She felt groggy. Probably because for the first time in months she'd slept deeply all through the night. Maybe it had been those three aspirins that had knocked her out so completely, she thought. Or maybe she'd simply felt safe here in this house that Chance Delacroix called home. Whatever the reason, Lucinda felt more rested than she had in a long time.

Throwing back the covers, she sat up and swung her legs over the side of the bed. Her ankle still looked swollen and was painfully sore when she attempted to move it in any direction, but at least the constant throbbing ache had stopped.

Carefully she raised herself off the bed and hopped on her good foot until she reached a pair of long, arched windows.

The view outside the paned glass surprised her as much as the sight of this house had last night. From what she could see the D Bar D wasn't just a fancy ranch house pretending to be a ranch. There were barns and sheds everywhere she looked and an endless maze of holding pens and corrals. Numerous herds of black Angus cattle stood huddled together in the falling snow. Some of the luckier ones were being driven by cowboys on horseback to a long feeding shed with a roof over it.

Lucinda peered closely at the cowboys, trying to see if Chance might be one of them, but they were too far away for a clear look. Which was just as well, she told herself, turning away from the window. She'd gone to sleep last night with the man on her mind, now he was right back on it again this morning. She didn't like the idea of thinking about Chance Delacroix that much, but that was hardly enough reason to make her stop.

Hopping back to the bed, she tried to assure herself that it wasn't strange that she found him attractive. Any woman with eyes would. On top of that, she'd never known a cowboy before, or any man who worked with animals and the outdoors. That intrigued her about him. That and a whole lot more if she were honest enough to admit it.

Lucinda was sitting on the side of the bed, rummaging through her purse for a powder compact when a light rap sounded on the door. She pulled on the blue robe Dee had brought to her last night and tied the sash before calling, "Come in."

A tall, young woman wearing a long corduroy skirt and matching rust-colored sweater entered the room. She was carrying a tray with an insulated coffeepot and a thin china cup. A warm smile spread across her face as she spotted Lucinda on the side of the bed.

"Good morning," she said cheerfully. "I'm Sarah Jane, Chance's sister. Sorry I didn't make it in to meet you last night. How are you feeling this morning? Did you sleep well?"

Obviously Sarah Jane was just as warm and gracious as her mother. "I'm feeling much better. Your brother told me it was your engagement party last night. I hope my being here didn't create a problem," Lucinda told her.

Sarah Jane laughed and Lucinda realized the woman was younger than herself, perhaps not much older than nineteen. Yet she seemed uncommonly poised for her age. She had copper red hair almost as long as Lucinda's. The natural curls were tied back at her nape with a black velvet ribbon, and just looking at this young woman made Lucinda feel very unkempt.

"Not in the least," Sarah Jane assured her. "We hardly ever have the treat of having visitors here on the D Bar D. I do wish the snow had held off for a while, though. Everyone got worried about the roads and left the party early."

She set the tray down on the nightstand. "Would you like me to help you walk to the bathroom?"

"Oh, yes!" Lucinda said with relief. "I was just sitting here wondering if I could make it across this big room."

As though she'd known her for years, Sarah Jane put her arm around the back of Lucinda's waist and gently helped her to stand on one foot. "Chance told us how he found your car. Lord, I'm glad I begged him to go after those lamb fries. Otherwise, you might have frozen out there!"

"I'm very grateful to him. To all of you for your kindness," Lucinda told her.

Sarah Jane waved away her thanks. "It's nothing. Really."

But it was something to Lucinda, who'd spent nearly all of her growing-up years in an orphanage. Without the kindness and generosity of strangers back then, she would have been lost and alone. The same way she would have been last night if Chance hadn't come to her rescue.

With Sarah Jane's help, Lucinda managed to walk to the bathroom. While she made use of the facilities, Sarah Jane stood outside the door and chatted.

"Doc says you should be walking fine by Christmas."

"Well, I guess that's something to look forward to," Lucinda said as cheerfully as she could. Though it was hard to look on the bright side when she knew her Christmas would be spent entirely alone.

There was a hairbrush on the vanity. Lucinda pulled it through her tangled hair. It needed shampooing terribly, but she supposed that could wait until she got to a motel room. Which might be as soon as this evening, if the weather cleared and the wrecker service delivered her car.

"Chance said you were from Chicago," Sarah Jane spoke up again. "Are you vacationing?"

"No." With her hair finally free of tangles and brushed away from her face, she moistened a washcloth with warm water and pressed it to her eyes. "I'm actually—moving."

"Oh, really? How exciting! I've lived in this same house ever since I was born. I can't wait to move."

Lucinda's mouth twisted wryly at Sarah Jane's comment. For so many years she'd longed to have a family and a real permanent home such as this. But that would be hard to explain to someone who'd never been without such things.

"You don't think you'll miss your mother and brother?"

"Oh, sure I will. But I'm only moving about five miles from here. If I want to visit, all I'll have to do is ride or drive over."

Lucinda couldn't imagine what it would feel like to have such a network of family and friends, to know that if she had any sort of crisis in her life, there would always be someone close to help her through it.

"I'm sure your family is pleased about that."

"Oh, yes. Especially Chance. He thinks I'm too young to be married anyway. And this way, he'll be able to keep an eye on me."

Lucinda frowned at her pale image in the mirror. "Doesn't that bother you?"

"Not really. Oh, he's overprotective most of the time. But he's only that way because he loves me."

Yeah, Lucinda thought wearily, she'd heard that all before. Each time she'd caught Richard watching her every move, he'd told her he was doing it because he loved her. Well, as far as Lucinda was concerned she could do without that sort of love.

Finished in the bathroom, Lucinda opened the door to find Sarah Jane waiting to help her back across the room. At the bed, she picked out a skirt and sweater from the things Dee had brought her last night and carried them behind a dressing screen.

Sarah Jane made herself at home on the foot of the bed. "What did you do back in Chicago, Lucy?"

"I design clothes."

Sarah Jane let out a small gasp of surprise. "Oh my, you must be very talented to make a living doing that. I mean, that's not the sort of thing just anybody can go out and do."

Lucinda pulled a rose-colored sweater over her head. It fell past her hips and over a full skirt printed with tiny matching roses. "Don't get me wrong, Sarah Jane, I'm only small-scale. But I sold enough things out of a little shop in Chicago to make a living for myself."

"Well, that's certainly a start! A pretty grand one, I'd say." She clapped her hands together. "Wait till Mother hears about this! She'll love it!"

Lucinda stepped from behind the screen and Sarah Jane immediately laughed. "I guess I'm a little taller than you."

Laughing with her, Lucinda glanced down at her borrowed clothes. "Only about five inches, but long hemlines are in style now. Especially when they hide a swollen ankle."

"If you'd rather, I could get you a pair of jeans," Sarah Jane offered.

"Oh no," Lucinda assured her. "The skirt is very nice. I love the colors."

"You look very pretty in it." Sarah Jane left her seat on the bed and began to carefully pull Lucinda's hair out from the neck band of the sweater.

Lucinda was touched by the simple gesture and wondered if it might have been like this if she'd had a sister. "Thanks," she murmured once Sarah Jane had freed her hair, then hobbled over to the dresser where she'd left her purse and what little makeup she carried in it.

While she dabbed on a bit of face powder and lipstick, Sarah Jane asked, "Are you married?"

Lucinda shook her head. The word *marriage* left her cold now. She knew she shouldn't feel that way. But she couldn't help herself. "No. I think it's not meant for me to be married."

Sarah Jane clucked her tongue, then laughed softly. "That's what Chance says, too. But I think he's wrong. I think you're probably wrong, too."

Lucinda smiled wanly. It was obvious that Sarah Jane was young and in love and marriage seemed like a bright, beautiful union of two hearts. But that wasn't the way it would have turned out for Lucinda.

A few minutes later, the two women left the bedroom and went down to the kitchen where Dee had a cup of coffee and a wooden cane waiting for Lucinda.

"I thought it would get you around until you're able to put a little more weight on your foot," she said of the cane.

Lucinda was once again amazed. These people didn't know her. They didn't know what sort of life she'd led, or what kind of person she might be. But they treated her warmly and generously just the same.

"Thanks, I'm sure it will be a big help," she said, taking a seat at the breakfast counter.

While she sipped the richly brewed coffee, Lucinda looked around the long room, which was actually part kitchen, part dining area. It was decorated with all sorts of Christmas items. There was everything from a tablecloth printed with prancing reindeer, to Santa Claus-shaped pot holders. Real spruce, pinecones and holly berries made up a huge centerpiece in the middle of the dining table, while poinsettia plants ranging from deep red to pale white sat on worktables, cabinet counters and atop the refrigerator.

"This is all so beautiful," Lucinda exclaimed. "I've never seen a kitchen decorated for Christmas before."

Dee smiled at Lucinda's awed expression. "After you drink your coffee, you should go in and look at the living room, while Sarah Jane and I get breakfast ready. Chance should be in from the feedlots soon and then we'll all eat.''

The rest of the house turned out to be just as beautifully decorated as the kitchen. She was staring up at the huge Virginia pine in the living room when Chance's voice sounded behind her.

"We normally don't put up the tree until a few days before Christmas, but this year we made an exception because of Sarah Jane's party.''

Lucinda turned to look at him and instantly felt her heart begin to hammer with foolish anticipation. She was glad to see him. There was no way she could deny it. Dee and Sarah Jane had been nice and helpful to her, but Chance was the one who'd gotten her out of the car and carried her through the snow, twice. He was her rescuer and she couldn't help but feel a little bit close to him.

"It's magnificent. Did you help decorate it?''

His gray eyes roamed over her rather than the tree. Lucinda didn't know if the path of his gaze was intentional or not. But either way, she felt touched by him.

"My job is to put on the lights. Mother and Sarah Jane do the rest.''

He was wearing jeans and boots and a dark blue denim shirt. At the open throat she could see the banded neck of a thermal undershirt, to help keep him warm. This morning he was wearing a black hat similar to the one he'd worn last night, only this one was stained around the band with dirt and sweat. The brim was bent in places and rolled up in a tighter curl on the sides. Lucinda thought the hat fit him perfectly. It had much more character than the one she'd seen on him last night. Maybe that was because she somehow knew this particular hat was probably always on his head or in his hands.

"I see you've been out working. Is the weather getting any better?"

He shrugged. "Well, it's not blizzard conditions anymore, but it is still snowing." He took a few steps toward her. "How's your ankle? Do you think you should be trying to hobble around on it this morning?"

"If it hurts, I'll quit," she assured him.

Chance was close enough to her now to see the infinite shades of green in her eyes, the smooth porcelain quality of her skin and the dusky pink color that stained her lips. He had a thousand things to do, but right now looking at her seemed to be the most important.

"You don't take orders very well, do you?"

Lucinda had never heard a true Texas accent until she'd driven into the state yesterday and stopped in Amarillo to eat and service her car. Yet none of the men she'd encountered there had sounded quite like Chance Delacroix. His voice was deep, rich and slow. It shivered over her, curled around her with a warmth all its own.

That warmth melted the cool distance she wanted to keep between them, and before she knew it, a smile was tilting the corners of her mouth. "Actually, I don't."

"Then how are you with invitations?"

Her eyebrows lifted. "You're inviting me somewhere?"

He held his arm out to her. "To breakfast. Have you ever eaten chorizo and eggs?"

She took his arm and instantly scolded herself for liking the feel of it beneath her hand. "No. I haven't."

"Do you like things hot?"

Just what sort of things? she wondered, and glanced up to see a grin on his face that could only be described as sexy. Before she could stop it, a deep blush of red swept across her cheeks.

"Your food, Lucy. Do you like it hot?"

"Sometimes. But I've never tried it for breakfast. Usually I'm in too big of a rush to eat anything in the mornings."

"Sounds like you've been living too fast," Chance said.

Lucinda had never considered her life fast. Back in Chicago she'd spent her days at work and her nights at home, alone. She'd certainly not had a man like Chance Delacroix inviting her to breakfast with him. And even if there had been an invitation from a man, Richard's stalking would have made it impossible for her to accept it.

Yet here she was in Texas, hanging on to Chance's big arm and blushing like a schoolgirl. Had she lost her mind? Or had she just now become brave enough to live again?

Chapter Four

Scrambled with Mexican sausage and served with soft tortillas, the eggs were very hot, and equally delicious. Instead of the small breakfast counter, the four of them ate at the dining table.

Lucinda sat at Sarah Jane's right and directly across the table from Chance. She caught his eyes on her often and, each time she did, it jolted her right down to her toes.

"Chance, did you know that Lucinda designs clothes?" Sarah Jane spoke up between bites of food. "She sold her things out of a shop in Chicago. Isn't that the most exciting thing you've ever heard?"

Chance glanced from his sister to Lucinda. "Is that what you were doing when you left Chicago?" he asked.

Lucinda nodded, wondering why she found it so difficult to think of Chance Delacroix as any other man. What was it about him that made her insides hot and shaky? Why did she notice every little thing about him?

She didn't know why she was intrigued by the way his black hair waved away from his forehead, the way his darkly tanned skin had been bitten by the cold wind and was now flushed red from the indoor heat. He hadn't shaved this morning and she could see his beard was black and heavy. If she were to rub her cheek against his, she knew it would scrape her skin. Yet she knew it would be a pleasant sensation.

"I—yes, I was," she answered as she desperately tried to shove aside the thoughts running through her head.

"Is that what you're planning to do when you get to—" His brows lifted in question. "You never did say where you were going, did you?"

Lucinda took a deep breath, then let it out slowly. She knew he was purposefully trying to pull information out of her. And she supposed she shouldn't blame him. If a stranger was staying in her house, she'd probably feel she was entitled to know a few things about the person. Still, she wasn't used to confiding anything to anyone. Especially these past months when she'd had to watch everything she'd said and done in fear that Richard might pick up the information through a mutual friend.

"No. I guess I didn't say," she told him.

Chance frowned and reached for his coffee cup. Across the table, Sarah Jane said to him, "Lucinda is moving."

"Moving? Where?" Dee asked curiously.

It was obvious she could no longer avoid their questions, and perhaps it wouldn't make any difference anyway. If she made it to California without Richard tracking her, then she could probably lose herself in one of the state's major cities.

"California," she answered. "I've always wanted to see the West Coast."

Chance eyed her over the rim of his coffee cup. "So you're going to design clothes and try to sell them out there?

Isn't that an iffy thing to do? If you were making a living in Chicago, looks like you'd want to stay where you already have customers who know you.''

Damn him, why did he have to be so smart and nosy? Dropping her eyes back to her plate, she scooped up a fork-ful of eggs and lifted them to her lips. ''I guess moving is a chancy thing to do. But I think my clothes will sell better out West. California's economy hasn't been all that good in the past few years and I think the women out there are looking for more affordable fashions.''

Pleased with her quick thinking, Lucinda chewed the eggs, then reached for her coffee. While she carefully sipped the rich brew, she felt Chance's gaze lingering on her. Was he suspicious of her, or did he merely like what he was looking at? Whatever the reason, Lucinda knew that she was definitely going to have to watch herself around the man.

''You might be right about that, Lucy,'' Dee spoke up. ''Course, around here, we women just go to the closest mall and buy our clothes off the rack. Unless there's a special occasion going on and then we have something made.''

''Like my wedding. I'm getting married in May,'' Sarah Jane said, her face suddenly glowing as she turned toward Lucinda. ''I've already chosen the fabric for my gown. I'd love you to take a look at it, Lucy. I'd value your opinion.''

Lucinda shook her head. ''I've never done bridal gowns before.''

''But I'm sure you know all about fabric and lines, how it will all look when it comes together. You—'' Sarah Jane stopped abruptly, then quickly asked Lucinda, ''Did you bring any of your work with you?''

''Yes, several pieces are in my car. The woman who worked as my seamstress is going to send the rest to me once I get settled.''

Sarah Jane turned a pleading look on her brother. "Chance, will you please go get Lucinda's cases from her car? I'm dying to see her work!"

Chance grimaced. "I've got cattle to feed, Sarah Jane. Several herds, in fact."

Sarah Jane pulled a face at him. "You have hired hands working, Chance. Surely they can make it without you for half an hour. Besides," she went on before Chance could argue, "if Lucinda is going to stay here with us, she needs her own things."

He turned a pointed look on Lucinda. "Is that right?"

When he looked at her, she couldn't think, much less know what she needed. "I—well, if the wrecker gets my car this afternoon there's no need for you to—"

"Lucy, don't you let him off the hook!" Sarah Jane practically shouted. "Mike's the only wrecker service around here for miles. It might be tomorrow, or the next day before he gets around to getting your car out of the ditch. Especially if he knows you're here on the ranch and not absolutely stranded."

But she *was* stranded, Lucinda thought. She looked to Chance. "Is she right? Could it be tomorrow before I can get my car?"

Chance nodded. "Possibly. It's still snowing outside."

"Forget about the snow, Lucy. Your foot is hurt. You can't go anywhere until it gets better." Dee spoke in a persuasive tone.

Never having had a family to ply her with opinions and advice, Lucinda had always made decisions on her own. It more than bewildered her to have the Delacroix taking control of her plans.

"I think I can drive if—"

"Hellfire, woman!" Chance suddenly barked. "Didn't you learn anything last night? There's at least three or four inches of packed snow and ice on the highways! How long do you think it would be before you'd wind up right back in the ditch?''

Lucinda might have made a foolish judgment in the weather last night, but that didn't mean she was stupid. She shot him an annoyed look. "Don't you people have snowplows out here?"

Frowning at her, he said, "I'm sure the road graders are out at work, but I imagine the snow is falling about as fast as they can push it off."

So that was that, Lucinda concluded. She was going to be here on the D Bar D whether she wanted to be or not. "Then it looks like I will need my suitcases."

Sarah Jane began to giggle. "You're not going to tell Lucy you have to work now, are you, Chance?"

Ignoring his sister, he said to Lucinda, "After breakfast I'll warm up the Jeep. Would you like to go with me?"

Go with him? She did, and she didn't.

The indecision must have shown on her face, because Chance went on before she could give him an answer. "You don't have to worry about wrecking again. We should be safe traveling in the Jeep."

Yes, but would it be safe traveling with him? she wondered. Aloud she said, "I'll be ready."

A half hour later, bundled in her long, red coat and a white woolen scarf, Lucinda stood beside Chance on the back porch and looked out at the Jeep. Between it and her were several yards of knee-deep snow. How was she going to hobble through all of that?

Reading her thoughts, Chance stooped over and lifted her into his arms. "Don't worry about my back," he said before she could put up a protest. "You hardly weigh more than a couple of sacks of good horse feed."

Instinctively Lucinda looped her arms around his neck and pressed her face dangerously close to his. "Good horse feed doesn't weigh the same as bad horse feed?" she couldn't help asking.

Chuckling, he stepped off the porch with her and into the deep snow. "No. Bad horse feed weighs more 'cause it has worms in it."

Beneath the brim of his Stetson, she could see the sky was lead gray and snow was falling thick and fast. She should have been worried at the sight. The more it snowed, the longer she would have to stay here on the ranch. Yet all she could think at the moment was that Chance didn't smell like soap or cologne. His scent was pure man and so intoxicating she hardly knew where she was until he'd placed her on the Jeep's bucket seat.

"Thank you," Lucinda murmured as he carefully pulled his arm from beneath her knees.

"You're welcome," he said lowly.

Her heart going in a mad gallop, Lucinda's eyes inched upward to find his face hovering just inches away from hers. The tempting sight crumbled her common sense. And though she knew it was crazy, more than anything she wanted to cup her palms against his jaws, feel his skin, his whiskers, draw his face to hers and kiss his lips.

"I think—" With one hand he reached above her head. The movement caused his face to dip even closer to hers. Lucinda drew in a sharp breath and gripped the edge of the seat. "You'd be safer belted in," he finished, drawing the belt across her lap.

"You're probably right." Her voice was barely above a whisper, but at some point during the past few minutes she'd forgotten to breathe.

As he snapped the seat belt against her tummy, she let out a long, burning breath, then waited until he'd stepped back from her before she drew in a fresh one.

You've gone crazy, Lucinda, she scolded herself after Chance had shut the door and gone around to climb into his own seat. She'd spent the better part of this whole year in misery because of a man. How could she look at Chance, a man she didn't really know, and feel such strong erotic urges?

"You've certainly got Sarah Jane stirred up," Chance told her as he carefully put the Jeep into motion. "If I hadn't agreed to go get your suitcases, she would have probably tried driving herself."

Even though Lucinda was wearing gloves, she jammed her hands down into the deep pockets of the coat. Maybe there, her fingers would forget all about touching Chance Delacroix.

"You make her sound headstrong."

Chance grunted. "She is at times. But I try my best to keep her reined in. Which hasn't always been easy to do. A brother isn't the same as a daddy. But I've tried to be both to Sarah Jane for the past ten years."

They were out of the ranch yard now and headed down the lane. Lucinda noticed it was lined on both sides by huge cottonwood trees. Like most of the other trees in this part of the country, the bare limbs had been permanently whipped to the north by the relentless winds. At the moment, the trees, as well as the railed fence that followed the arrow-straight road, were decorated with snow.

"Your father has been dead that long?" she asked.

He didn't look at her. Nor did his expression alter as he answered, "Yes. He died suddenly. An aneurysm in the brain. He was still a young man at the time."

Even though his face didn't show it, Lucinda could hear the pain of loss in Chance's voice, and it told her that he'd obviously been close to his father.

"I'm sorry you lost him. But at least you have your mother. And she's still a young, vibrant woman."

A fond smile crossed Chance's face. "Mother is one of a kind." He glanced at Lucinda. "And she very much wants you to stay on the ranch for the holidays."

Lucinda pushed her hands deeper into the coat pockets. "What about you? Dr. Campbell said you were the top dog around here."

Chance laughed and Lucinda felt herself melting at the warm sound. "Being the top dog doesn't necessarily mean anything. Not when the dog has two women to keep happy."

Sighing, Lucinda looked out at the golden plains that were now covered in a sea of white. It was a very beautiful sight to Lucinda. But last night she'd learned just how harsh and unpredictable this country could be in spite of that beauty.

"I wouldn't blame you if you weren't keen about me staying in your home," she told him. "For all you know I could have a very sordid past."

Chance didn't believe her past was anything close to sordid. At least he didn't want to think it was. However, she did seem secretive about herself. But rather than putting Chance off, her evasiveness had only made him more intrigued with her.

"Are you warning me that I might wake up one morning and find that you've skipped out with all the silverware and every last Christmas gift under the tree?"

Lucinda couldn't help but laugh at his ridiculous question. "Maybe I should wait until you open your gifts first. I might not bother taking the things I don't like."

"Well, I don't imagine you'd like the box of farrier tools Mother got me. Fashion designers probably don't shoe horses."

Smiling, she glanced at him from the corner of her eye. "How do you know that's what she got you?"

"Because I told her to."

Lucinda shook her head with wry disbelief. "That couldn't be any fun. Your gifts are supposed to be a surprise."

Chance kept a tight grip on the steering wheel as the Jeep plowed through the deeply rutted snow. "Oh, you can rest assured Mother will have plenty of other surprises under the tree."

Yes, Lucinda figured Dee was the sort of person who loved Christmas and gave as much as she could to everyone around her.

"What are you going to get for Christmas, Lucinda?" he asked a bit impishly. "Have you already told Santa what you want?"

If there truly was a Santa Claus, Lucinda would have simply told him she wanted someone to love her, to share her life and make a family with. But the possibility of there being a real Santa out there somewhere was about as remote as her finding a man she could trust enough to give her heart to.

"Santa forgot about me a long time ago. So I guess I'll—" Actually Lucinda wouldn't be getting anything for Christmas. But she didn't want to admit that to Chance. It was too painful to think about, much less share with a man who'd never known what it was like to be really and truly alone. "I'll have to wait and see what my friend in Chicago sends me. Probably a box of chocolates. She thinks I'm too thin."

She. Chance shouldn't have been so pleased to hear that Lucinda's friend was female. But he was. He couldn't help wanting to believe that she was completely unattached. He wanted to know that every time he looked at her, he wasn't looking at another man's woman.

"Last night I got the distinct impression you were running from Chicago," he said.

Inside the coat pockets, Lucinda's hands tightened into fists. Her gaze remained fixed on the windshield. "I didn't run from Chicago. I simply left."

"And you left because of a man. Didn't you?"

Was she that transparent? Lucinda wondered. Dear Lord, had he been able to read the wanton thoughts going on in her head a few minutes ago when he'd set her in the Jeep?

Slowly she moistened her lips, then glanced over at him. He was watching the road ahead, but she knew he was expecting her to answer. She also knew that if she didn't give him one, he'd continue to pester her about it.

"What makes you think I left Chicago because of a man?"

His mouth twisted. "Because I figure you had to work long and hard to build up the sort of clientele you need to make a living in your business. You wouldn't just up and leave all that for a change of scenery."

"I told you—"

"I know what you said at breakfast. But I wasn't born yesterday, Lucy. You might have fooled Mother and Sarah Jane with all that business about the economy, but you didn't fool me."

Turning her head, she frowned at him. "I didn't know cowboys played detective."

"Now you're being flip," he accused.

"And you're being nosy," she shot back.

He suddenly braked the Jeep to a halt and Lucinda looked out to see they'd reached her wrecked car. Good, she thought with relief, maybe he'd go after her cases now and let this whole conversation drop.

Her hopes were quickly dashed when Chance squared around in the seat to face her.

"Maybe I am nosy," he conceded. "But I just don't see how running across the country could cure you of a broken heart."

He thought she had a broken heart? Before she could stop herself, she let out a caustic laugh. "I'm not moving across country because of my heart. I—" She broke off, then heaved out a sigh as Chance patiently folded his arms across his chest.

"Yes?" he prompted.

Why was he doing this? she wondered. She was just someone he and his family had befriended. In a few days she'd be out of their lives. It shouldn't matter to him why she'd left Chicago. But it seemed to, and that shook her.

As far as she knew, no one had ever really cared what happened to Lucinda Lambert. Some, like Richard, had pretended to. Others, like those at the orphanage, had cared for her because it was their job. So why should she think this man was any different?

Tossing her hair away from her face, she let out a weary sigh. "I left Chicago because—well, a whole lot of bad memories were there and I wanted to get away from them. I want to start somewhere fresh."

"I can understand that," he replied, his voice much softer than it had been moments ago.

Could he really understand? she wondered as her eyes slowly searched his strong face. She couldn't imagine him ever feeling so desperate that he wanted to leave his home. He'd always had a family who loved him.

Swallowing down the sudden lump that had collected in her throat, Lucinda turned her gaze back outside the windshield. "Last year at this time I was engaged to be married."

His jaw tightened. "What happened?"

She shrugged as though none of it mattered, but Chance could tell from the distant look on her face that she was back in a painful time and place. He could only wonder what sort of man could have hurt this woman. Moreover, what kind of man could ever have given her up?

"Things didn't work out. He was—very possessive and I—well, I broke off our engagement and ended the relationship."

She'd pulled her hands out of her pockets and removed her gloves. Now they were on her lap, clasped together so tightly her knuckles were white. Chance wanted to reach over, unclench her hands and press them between the two of his. He wanted to reassure her, make her smile, make her glad that she was with him and not that man she'd once promised herself to.

"Do you regret that it's over?"

Chance's question pulled her gaze back around to him. If only he knew how desperately she wished the whole thing with Richard was finally and truly over.

"No," she said with a shake of her head. "It was the only choice I had. Now I want to put all of that behind me."

Maybe her heart wasn't broken and maybe she was moving simply to have a fresh start. But he wasn't blind. The shadows that haunted her eyes told him she was troubled about something and that bothered Chance. More than he cared to admit.

He opened the door, but before he climbed to the ground, he looked at her and said, "Then I hope you can leave all those memories back there, Lucy. I really do."

As Lucinda watched Chance wade through the snow to her car, she realized she was shaking. It wasn't strange for a woman to want to kiss a man as attractive as Chance Delacroix. But now her wants were going a step further. She'd told him a part of her past and had wanted to tell him more. She'd wanted to lay her head on his chest, hang on to his broad shoulders and tell him the fear and helplessness she'd been living with these past months. What did it mean?

Don't think about what it means, she silently whispered. Don't think about him or the way he smells and looks and talks. Just because he was a big, physically tough man didn't mean he could protect her, or that he'd even want to.

No, she thought, the only person who could take care of her and keep her safe was herself. She had to remember that.

Chapter Five

"Lucinda, these are the most gorgeous things I've ever seen in my life! Look at this blue crepe suit, Mother. Wouldn't it be great for traveling?"

The three women were in Lucinda's bedroom, where Sarah Jane had scattered Lucinda's fashions all over the bed, dressing table and a stuffed armchair.

Dee picked up the Wedgwood blue jacket lying on the bed and held it out in front of her.

"It's very nice," she agreed. "What size is it, Lucy?"

"An eight, I think."

Dee shook her head. "Forget it, Sarah Jane. That's too small for you."

"Oh, but I love it. I wish you could make another for me," she told Lucinda, who was sitting in a nearby rocking chair with her injured ankle propped on a footstool. "Or do you ever duplicate your pieces?"

"Of course I do. But I didn't actually sew—"

Before Lucinda could finish, Sarah Jane whirled around to her mother. "Can I have the suit, Mother? Better yet," she said, her voice suddenly squeaking with excitement, "can Lucinda design a few more things for me to wear on my honeymoon?"

Dee cast her daughter a doubtful glance. "The cost, Sarah Jane. We're already spending so much for the wedding."

"I'll leave something off," Sarah Jane quickly suggested. "Like the band and the champagne. We can dance to recorded music and drink fruit punch."

Dee groaned helplessly. "I'm sure the men will all love fruit punch."

"We'll give the men beer. That's what all of them are used to drinking anyway."

Dee laughed. "You're right about that. But serving beer at a wedding? People will say we're uncouth."

Sarah Jane picked up a green silk dress and waltzed over to a cheval mirror. "Since when have we Delacroix worried about what other people say? And James certainly won't care, especially when he sees how beautiful I look in the clothes Lucinda designs for me."

Tossing the dress over her arm, Sarah Jane went to kneel beside Lucinda's chair. "You will design some things for me, won't you? I'd be forever in your debt!"

How could Lucinda say no? Chance had rescued her from a potentially dangerous situation and his mother and sister had already gone out of their way to make her feel at home. Besides all of that, Sarah Jane was so young and beautiful and excited about getting married that Lucinda didn't want to be the one to spoil anything for her.

"You'd have to find your own seamstress. I'm not that good at it," Lucinda told her.

"There's Margie. Over by Friona," Dee said thoughtfully. "She's very professional. And in the end, we'd probably save money having the clothes made, rather than buying out of those expensive boutiques in Amarillo or Fort Worth."

Lucinda smiled at Sarah Jane, who was breathlessly waiting for her answer.

"I'd be glad to do it. On one condition," Lucinda added.

Sarah Jane clapped her hands together gleefully and Lucinda wondered sadly if she would ever feel that lighthearted and happy. Would there ever come a time in her life when she'd be planning her own wedding to a man who really loved her?

"What's the condition?" Dee asked.

Lucinda looked at the older woman. "That I do a dress for you, too, Dee. And that you'll accept my work as a Christmas gift."

"That's asking too much!" Dee began with a shake of her head, but Sarah Jane was already flinging her arms around Lucinda and smacking a kiss on her cheek.

"Oh, thank you, Lucy, you're wonderful!" Sarah Jane exclaimed.

Lucinda had been praised for her work before. Coming from paying customers, the compliments had meant much to her. But seeing the genuine joy on Sarah Jane's face, the gratefulness on Dee's, stung Lucinda's eyes with tears.

Clearing her throat, she warned jokingly, "Maybe you should see how the clothes turn out before you call me wonderful."

Sarah Jane went back to the bed, held up the Wedgwood jacket and sighed with pure appreciation. "Just wait till Chance hears what you're doing. He'll probably kiss you, too, for saving him so much money."

Lucinda couldn't stop the blush she felt creeping across her cheeks. The idea of kissing her would more than likely never enter Chance's head. But it had definitely gotten into hers and she couldn't seem to get it out.

"That would be the day," Dee said glumly. "As far as I know it's been years since Chance kissed a woman."

The happy glow on Sarah Jane's face suddenly vanished. "That's true, Mother. I guess he—well, with everything that happened with Jolene. He doesn't want anything to do with women."

With a deeply resigned sigh, Dee swiped her tousled red hair off her forehead. "Well, he's wrong and I've told him so. But hearing it from me hasn't done any good."

Lucinda's gaze swung curiously from mother to daughter. Who was this woman they were talking about? And why had she ruined Chance's interest in women? The questions whirled around in her head, demanding an answer.

"Was Jolene an old flame of Chance's?" she finally asked.

Dee shook her head. Sarah Jane said, "Jolene was Chance's wife."

Later that night, Lucinda sat quietly in her room near a window overlooking an east pasture. A sketch pad lay open on her lap, while several colored pencils were scattered atop a table beside her chair. For the past hour she'd been trying to concentrate and do a little work toward the clothes she'd promised Sarah Jane. But her mind refused to cooperate. All she could think about was Chance and that he'd once been married.

Where was Jolene now, she wondered. And why had the marriage ended? Lucinda had been about to ask those very questions this afternoon, but the phone had rung, interrupting the moment. Sarah Jane had rushed out of the room to answer it. Dee had quickly fled, too, saying she had to check on the beans she'd left cooking on the stove.

By the time things had quieted back down, Lucinda had decided not to bring up the subject again. Sarah Jane and Dee would probably think it odd that she would be that interested in Chance's past life.

And it was odd, she told herself as she looked up from the sketch pad for the umpteenth time. Chance was none of her business. Nor would he ever be. The sooner she got that through her head, the better off she'd be.

A light knock suddenly sounded on the door. Grateful for the interruption, Lucinda called, "Come in."

To her surprise it was Chance who strolled into the room. He'd changed from the denim shirt he'd been wearing this morning. Now a plaid flannel shirt of reds and greens flapped open against his thermal undershirt. The battered hat was gone. Without it, she could see that his black hair was shiny wet and combed neatly to one side. Lucinda could only think how solid he looked, how strikingly male, and how just looking at him made her stomach flutter.

"I wanted to see if you're ready for supper," he said.

Quickly Lucinda placed her sketchbook on the table with her pencils and reached for the cane Dee had given her. "I hadn't noticed the time. I hope you haven't been waiting on me."

Chance watched her hobble toward him. She seemed determined to get around on her own steam and he liked that independence about her. Especially when he knew how much pain it must be costing her to walk.

"It's only you and me," he said.

A look of utter surprise came over her face. "It is?"

Chance's mouth twisted wryly. The last thing he'd wanted was to be left alone with Lucy. Or so he'd thought. Now that he was looking at her, he was glad the house had emptied, except for the two of them. "James has taken Sarah Jane over to his parents tonight."

"On these roads?"

"It's not that far and he has a four-wheel-drive vehicle," Chance explained. "As for Mother, she just left with Doc. It seems they have a mutual friend who needs his medical attention."

So it was just the two of them, Lucinda thought, trying not to let the idea of being alone with him shake her. After all, she wasn't afraid of him. On the contrary, she instinctively knew she could trust her very life with him. But what about her? She couldn't even look at him without going a little bit crazy!

"I see. Well, I'll be perfectly fine making myself a sandwich. You don't have to go out of your way for me."

He took her arm and guided her from the bedroom. "Supper is already on the table. Chili beans, corn bread and apple cobbler."

"Did you cook it?"

He chuckled and Lucinda decided the sound was as warm as the feel of his fingers on her arm.

"No. My cooking is limited to opening cans or frozen dinners."

Because of her ankle, she was forced to walk slowly toward the kitchen. Chance seemed content to go at her pace and lend her the support of his arm. Last night he'd told her he was used to taking care of women. Tonight she realized he'd probably been speaking the truth.

"I guess it wouldn't be the macho thing for a cowboy to cook," she replied.

"The reason this cowboy didn't learn was because he never had time."

They reached the kitchen, but Chance didn't release his hold on her until she was securely settled in one of the chairs.

As she waited for him to take his own seat, Lucinda thought about the tiny apartment she'd had in Chicago. She'd rarely cooked there, and when she had, it had been simple things. There hadn't been much point in cooking a meal just for herself. Most of the time she'd simply settled for something from a nearby deli. But being here with Chance like this made her realize how lonely and isolated her life had become.

"What about you, Lucy? Can you cook?"

She shrugged one shoulder then the other as he filled her bowl with chili beans. "A little. The nuns in the orphanage would take us into the kitchen at times and teach us basic things."

He handed the bowl to her. "I remember you said you didn't have family. You grew up in an orphanage?"

She nodded. "I can only guess that my mother must have been Catholic. When she was killed in an auto accident, I was placed in a Catholic orphanage in Chicago."

"How old were you then?"

"Going on five, I think."

Surprised, he glanced at her. "So you can remember your mother?"

Nodding, Lucinda took a square of corn bread from a cloth-lined basket. "I can remember a few things about her. She was blond and pretty. She always smelled like flowers and at bedtime she sang lullabies to me."

Chance couldn't imagine how sad it must be for her to only have those few precious things to remember her mother by. He'd had years with his father and with them so many wonderful memories. He'd been young when he'd lost his father. Yet compared to Lucinda's life, he'd been very blessed.

"What about your father?" he asked after he'd taken a few bites from his bean bowl.

Lucinda's eyes dropped to the tabletop. "As far as I know, I never had one. My mother was never married."

Sensing her awkwardness, Chance said, "That's nothing to be ashamed of. You were just an innocent child."

The gentleness in his voice brought her eyes up to his. She smiled wanly, "I'm not ashamed. I'm just not used to talking about these things with anyone."

There was an insulated pot of coffee on the table. Chance filled two cups and pushed one over to her. "What about your friends back in Illinois? You didn't talk to them about growing up in an orphanage?"

Lucinda took a bite of the beans, then tried the corn bread. Maybe if she kept her mind on the food, she could forget about how good he looked sitting across from her with the dim light throwing shadowy angles over his face. Maybe if she kept talking, she wouldn't think about how quiet the house was and that the two of them were completely alone.

"Chance, except for Molly, most of my friends weren't family-oriented people like you. Whether I had a father, or grew up in an orphanage didn't really interest them."

"Some friends," Chance muttered.

"At least they didn't judge me because of it."

"And you think I do?"

As her eyes connected with his, Lucinda felt something inside slipping away, leaving a part of her exposed to him. "No. I think you've never known anyone like me before."

She was right about that, Chance thought. None of the women he knew would take off driving across the country by themselves. None of them were as beautiful. And certainly none of them stirred him the way she did.

"You mean someone who doesn't have a list of aunts, uncles and cousins a mile long?" he asked.

She nodded and he grinned at her. "Well, think of all the money you save each Christmas by not having to buy ties and fruitcakes for them."

He truly wasn't looking down on her because she didn't come from a long family lineage. Knowing that warmed Lucinda's heart and drew her to him in spite of all the warnings going off in her head.

They continued to eat and talk of the weather and the stress it put on the cattle. Afterward, Chance carried their coffee into the living room, where the lights were twinkling brightly on the Christmas tree.

Standing beside it, Lucinda breathed in the faint scent of pine and took pleasure in looking at all the ornaments hanging from the branches. Many of them were obviously old and a little ragged. A little brown teddy bear had a missing ear, and a toy soldier had lost the end of his rifle, but she knew that being perfect had little to do with finding a place on the Delacroix's Christmas tree.

One particular glass ball had been glued with rows of colored rice and macaroni. She glanced over at Chance, who'd taken a seat in a recliner. "I'll bet you made this when you were about eight years old."

He rose from the chair and came to look. "That's my work all right. I was a trusty Cub Scout then. We made those ornaments to give to our mothers. I guess it's pretty obvious that Dee is sentimental."

She was beginning to think that he was sentimental, too, but she didn't say so. On the outside he was a tough cowboy, and she didn't expect a man like him would appreciate her insinuating that he had a soft spot.

"If I'm ever lucky enough to have a child who gives me an ornament for Christmas, I'll be just as sentimental about it as your mother," Lucinda told him.

As Chance watched a wistful sort of yearning come over her face, he felt ashamed of himself. Which didn't make sense. It wasn't his fault that Lucinda had grown up without her mother or any sort of family to share Christmas with. Still he couldn't help thinking of all the times he'd felt bitter about losing Jolene and their newborn daughter. Many times he'd felt as if he were the only person who'd ever suffered that much loss and loneliness. Lucinda was making him see just how wrong he'd been.

"Mother told me about the clothes you're planning to do for her and Sarah Jane. It's a very generous thing for you to do."

He was standing so close to her that her shoulder was brushing his chest, and even though she wasn't looking directly up at him, Lucinda knew his eyes were gliding over her lips and throat and downward to where her sweater clung to her breasts.

The feel of that hot gaze traveling over her left Lucinda's knees spongy and made her voice unusually husky when she spoke. "It's not that big of a deal. I'm not an Anne Klein or Liz Claiborne."

One corner of his mouth curled in a half grin. "No. You're Lucy. Maybe someday we'll see that name on a famous perfume."

Lucinda was trembling inside, and she wondered if Chance could see the pulse pounding at the side of her neck. Did he have any idea of the chaos he made of her senses?

"Then you don't mind about the clothes? Sarah Jane actually thought you'd be pleased because it will save you money."

His expression was suddenly full of amusement. "I'm sure she probably made me out to be a miser."

"No," Lucinda replied, then felt her face growing warmer with each passing second. "She didn't say anything of the sort. She said you'd probably kiss me."

Disbelief widened his eyes. "Kiss you? She said that?"

He sounded incredulous and Lucinda couldn't help but feel a little insulted. Was the idea of kissing her that horrible to him? "Uh—yes, because you'd be so grateful. But then your mother said no, you wouldn't kiss me because of Jolene."

Lucinda bit down on her lip, but it was too late. The words were already out.

His expression remained oddly fixed as he stared at her, then finally his eyelids drooped until he was watching her through two narrow slits. As she waited for him to say something, anything to break the crackling silence, Lucinda's heart began to pound so loud it roared in her ears.

"Well, she was wrong," he suddenly growled.

"Wrong? Who?" she asked breathlessly.

"My mother."

Before she could untangle the meaning of his words, Chance grabbed her shoulders and pulled her to him.

"If she thinks I won't kiss you, then she's going senile."

"Chance—"

His name was all she managed to get out before his head bent down to hers. Knowing he was going to kiss her, Lucinda braced herself for a quick smack on the lips. It didn't happen.

Long seconds began to tick away as his arms moved around her, drew her against him, then locked her there.

While his lips tasted, feasted on the full softness of hers, Lucinda felt herself being tugged to a place she'd never been, a hidden, exciting place where a mystical, intoxicating warmth seeped into her bones.

She clung to his shoulders as though he were the only solid thing in the world and moaned silently with regret when he finally lifted his lips from hers.

Chance had only meant to take one sweet, little taste of her lips. Now as he looked down into her flushed face, he felt dazed, rocked to the very soles of his feet by what had just happened between them.

"Do—uh, you always make a point of proving your mother wrong?"

Her voice was husky and trembling and he realized the sound of it was as alluring to him as the closeness of her just-kissed mouth.

"What do you think?" he murmured, his arms still anchoring the soft warmth of her body against his.

She thought if he really hadn't kissed a woman in years, then his memory of how to do it had certainly come to life a few moments ago.

"I think you're the sort of man who'd take on any challenge."

His brows lifted with wry speculation. "And you think kissing a woman is a challenge for me?"

"Yes. From what your mother said—"

Without warning, he released his grip on her waist and stepped back. "Dee had no business saying anything about Jolene to you!"

"And you think what you did to me a few moments ago *was* your business?" she asked, incredulous that he was displaying such anger over a wife who had obviously been out of his life for a long time.

"I wasn't in that kiss alone and you know it!"

He was right. There was no use denying that she'd been just as much a part of the kiss as he'd been. But he'd started it, and she wanted to know why.

"What difference does it make if your mother brought up Jolene's name? Is it supposed to be a secret that you two were once married?"

His face was suddenly a stony mask. "No. It isn't a secret. But all of that was—that's my private life. It's not something I share with anyone."

He couldn't have said anything that could have hurt Lucinda more. But then she'd asked for it, she told herself.

Turning slightly away from him, Lucinda stared with burning eyes at the ornament Chance had made for his mother so many years ago. She was stupid, she realized, to think she could ever mean that much to anyone.

"Well, I know what you're trying to say. I don't normally share my mother's death or the fact that I was raised in an orphanage with anyone, either. I guess I just had a momentary lapse with you." Stepping around him, she started out of the room. "If you'll excuse me, I'll get back to my work."

As Chance watched her limp away, her head up, her long hair swinging against her back, he hated himself. He'd never meant to hurt her, damn it! But Jolene was—dead, he forced himself to finish. When was he ever going to be able to put her memory to rest?

"Lucinda, wait!"

She didn't stop. Not until his hand came down on her shoulder. She looked up at him then, her expression as cool and distant as she could make it.

Chance's features twisted with anguish. "Look, I didn't mean that the way it sounded."

"Yes. You meant it."

He let out a long breath. "Okay. So maybe I did. But I was wrong."

Surprised by his admission, she turned around to face him. "No. I was wrong, Chance. I was wrong to think that one little kiss between us gave me any rights to bring up any woman in your past."

One little kiss? Is that how she thought of the embrace they'd shared? It had seemed more like instant combustion to Chance.

"But I expected you to tell me about yourself. And then I—" The frustration of wanting to make her understand made him shake his head. "I'm not used to talking about Jolene with anyone."

She shook her hair back away from her face. Chance watched a strand of it slide against the peak of her breast, then finally settle against her arm.

"Why not?" she asked.

During those moments Lucinda had been in his arms, Chance had forgotten all about Jolene. His mind had emptied of everything except for the taste of Lucinda's lips, the feel of her warm curves pressed against him. And he supposed that was the thing that had really angered him. He'd finally met a woman who could make him forget Jolene and he felt very guilty about that.

Releasing a tired breath, he said, "Because, like you, I don't want to look at painful memories."

She should have never started this conversation, Lucinda realized. Because now she was seeing more than just a cowboy who'd rescued her from a wrecked car. He was a man who'd once loved and lost, a man who wanted to keep his thoughts and his heart to himself. A man she was becoming hopelessly attracted to.

"You must have cared for her deeply," she murmured.

"I did care for her. But that didn't keep her from dying less than a year after we were married."

His words literally stunned the breath from Lucinda. The last thing she'd expected to hear was that Chance had been widowed. He must have been devastated.

"I'm sorry," she said, her voice barely above a whisper.

Chance was sorry, too, he realized. Sorry that he was afraid to take Lucinda back in his arms and let himself forget the past.

Shrugging, he said, "Yeah. Well, you wanted to know. Now you do."

She didn't know everything. Especially why he'd kissed her so passionately, but Lucinda wasn't going to remind him of that. She was going to put the whole thing down to a sudden whim and do her best to forget that she'd ever spent one moment in Chance Delacroix's arms.

"So now we're even. You've told me all about you and I've told you all about me," she said. Then forcing a smile on her face, she added, "And now I really am going back to my room. I promised your mother and sister some new clothes and I want to make sure they get them before I leave."

Chance watched her limp out of the room and, as he did, it dawned on him that he didn't want her to go. Not because his mother and sister were gone and the house was quiet. He simply wanted to have her in the same room with him. He wanted to be able to look at her, talk to her. *And touch her.*

Damn it, Chance, didn't you learn anything tonight? he asked himself. Kissing Lucinda hadn't turned out to be a simple meeting of their lips. It had been the meeting between a man and a woman, a precious glimpse of what could be.

But Chance knew what love could be. When it filled your heart the whole world was a magical place. Once it was gone, life became a living hell.

Chapter Six

The next morning Lucinda rose long before dawn, took a quick shower, then dressed in a pair of winter white corduroy pants and a cowl-necked, emerald green sweater.

After brushing and tying her towel-dried hair back from her face with a green velvet ribbon, she left the bedroom and headed to the kitchen.

She found it as dark and quiet as the rest of the house. Obviously the Delacroix family didn't rise quite this early in the morning, Lucinda decided as she flipped on a light over the kitchen sink.

Yesterday she'd learned where the coffee makings were so she quickly started a pot dripping, then went to look out the plate glass door leading onto the back porch.

Cupping her hands around her face and eyes, she could see the sky was clear and twinkling with stars. The white snow covering the ground gave off an eerie illumination, allowing her to see as far out as the barns and feedlots.

Sarah Jane had told her that in the spring and summer months, hundreds of acres of grain were grown in the nearby area, turning the fields into a sea of green. Right now it was hard to imagine the sight. Just placing her hands against the glass door told Lucinda the temperature outside was probably in the single digits.

The sound of the coffeepot gurgling its last few drops called her back over to the cabinet area. She filled a mug then poured in a bit of half-and-half cream she'd found in the refrigerator.

Lucinda drank the first few sips standing beside the cabinet before she carried her cup over to the breakfast counter and sank down onto one of the stools.

Even though she'd gone to bed early, she felt tired this morning. But that was hardly surprising when she'd spent the better part of the night flopping from one side of the mattress to the other.

No matter how hard she'd tried, she couldn't quit thinking about Chance, how distant he'd been because she'd mentioned Jolene and the expression on his face when he'd told her that his wife had died.

Lucinda could come to only one conclusion. Chance had never stopped loving the woman. Even though she was dead, she was still living in Chance's heart. It was no wonder he hadn't kissed anyone in years, she thought. He probably saw it as cheating on Jolene's memory.

Well, she wasn't going to be the one to tell him he was living in the past. She had her own problems to think about. She certainly didn't want to compound them by letting Chance get under her skin. It was bad enough to be running from one man, she didn't think she could survive two.

The unwelcome thought of Richard reminded Lucinda that she hadn't yet called Molly. She glanced at her wristwatch, then at the phone sitting on the bar a few feet down from her.

Her friend would be up now, getting her husband off to work and her children ready for school. Lucinda still had the kitchen to herself, so she wouldn't have to be worried about what she could safely say in front of the Delacroix family.

Before she could change her mind, she moved to the end of the bar and punched the operator for a collect call.

A few seconds later, Molly was squealing in her ear. "Lucy! Where in the world are you? I've been worried out of my mind!"

"I'm sorry, Molly. I meant to call you last night, but I—got sidetracked. I thought I'd catch you before you headed out to work this morning."

Molly breathed a long sigh of relief. "It's a good thing you did. I've been trying to decide whether to contact the police—"

"Molly, no! God forbid! You know Richard would be the first one to start looking for me!"

"I know. I know," she quickly assured Lucinda. "That's why I've tried to keep patient. So where are you now?"

"Actually, I'm stranded."

"Stranded! Lucy, come to your senses and catch a plane back to Chicago."

"Never. I'm not about to go back to that life." Especially now that she'd met the Delacroix and glimpsed for herself what living within a family really meant. She had to go on to California and hope that someday she'd have a real Christmas tree with ornaments made by her own children. And under the tree, she'd have gifts wrapped with love.

"Look, I'm fine, Molly. I'm staying with a family south-west of Amarillo. The way things stand right now, my car is wrecked, my ankle is sprained and the highways are covered with ice and snow. It looks like I'll be here for a few days. Possibly until after Christmas."

Molly groaned loudly. "You're staying with a family you don't even know? My lord, Lucy, don't they have motels out there?"

Lucinda realized the whole thing probably sounded strange to Molly, who considered a ten-mile trip to her mother's house an adventure. "The way things happened I couldn't make it to a motel. Besides, the Delacroix are very nice people. Their home is a big ranch called the D Bar D."

"You're on a ranch with real cows and cowboys?"

Lucinda couldn't help but laugh. Molly made it sound as though being on a ranch was the next thing to visiting Hollywood.

"That's right," Lucinda told her, then gave her the ranch's phone number just in case the other woman needed to contact her. "Now I'd better get off the line. I'm running up your bill."

"When can I expect to hear from you again?" Molly wanted to know.

"I'll call when I leave here. And Molly, if Richard happens to come snooping around, don't even hint that you know where I am."

"You know me better than that," Molly assured her. "I'll act like you haven't even left the city."

"Thank you, Molly."

"You can thank me by taking care of yourself," the other woman said.

"Don't worry about me. Once I get my car back and head on to California things will all work out." Footsteps suddenly sounded behind her. Lucinda looked over her shoulder to see Chance entering the room. "Uh, I've got to go, Molly. Have a good Christmas."

Before Molly could make a reply, she quickly slapped down the receiver and turned to Chance. "Good morning," she said. "You're up early."

He glanced pointedly at her, then the telephone. "Obviously not as early as you."

Before Lucinda could stop it, a flush of heat spread over her face. Damn him! He made her feel like a little girl caught with her finger in the sugar bowl.

"I guess I should have asked about using the phone first. But I called collect. So I thought—"

Frowning, he turned toward the coffeepot. "I'm not worried about the cost. I was only wondering who you'd be calling at such an early hour. Since you don't have family—"

"That was—my friend, Molly. Well, actually she's more than a friend. She was my seamstress. I promised to keep in close contact with her until I reached California."

"I see."

No, he couldn't really see, Lucinda thought, as she watched him reach for a mug. He didn't know that Molly was concerned for her safety, any more than he knew what it was like to have someone torture him with threats, to play sick games with his mind until it was impossible for him to eat, sleep or make sense of anything.

Chance poured the mug full of coffee then carried it over to where she sat at the breakfast counter. "Do you usually get up this early?" he asked.

She nodded. "During the workweek."

She didn't add that she'd gotten up this morning because it had been useless to remain in bed when she couldn't sleep. The tired lines on her face had probably already told him she'd spent a restless night.

"What about you? Is this your regular rising time?"

"Yeah. I like to have enough time to feed the horses before breakfast."

Propping her elbows on the breakfast bar, Lucinda leaned forward to put him out of the line of her vision. Yet her attempt to keep her eyes off him didn't work. Before she could stop herself, her head was turning to look at him. And blast it all, he still looked as damnably handsome as he had last night.

He was dressed similarly to yesterday, only this morning his shirt was black denim with pearl snaps. The top two at the throat were undone, giving her a view of his undershirt. Something about the white fabric lying against his darkly tanned throat struck her with the unexplainable urge to lean toward him. More than anything, she wanted to lay her hands upon his chest and slowly open the remaining snaps holding his shirt together. She wanted to push the tough denim aside and feel the soft cotton and warm muscles she knew she'd find beneath it.

"I have twenty head right now," he went on, unaware of the direction Lucinda's thoughts had taken. "All of them what we call 'using' horses. It costs like hell to feed that many, but I couldn't run the ranch without them. The D Bar D covers more than four thousand acres. That equals a lot of ground and cattle to look after. I know many ranchers use four-wheelers now to do some of the things horses do. But I don't cotton to those things."

Clearing her throat, she looked away from him, then pressed her fingers against her eyes. What was the matter with her? She thought she'd learned her lesson last night.

"You, uh, prefer the traditional ways," she said as she did her best to collect her thoughts.

"In the case of horses, I do."

And what about women, and marriage, and babies? she wanted to ask him, then gave herself another mental shake.

Chance had already been married once, and from the way he'd acted last night he wasn't about to love, honor and cherish any woman except his dead wife. The idea left a flat feeling inside of her.

"I'd like to see your horses sometime before I leave the ranch. Would you mind showing them to me?"

He looked at her with raised eyebrows. "I'm surprised you asked."

She frowned at him. "Why? Because I'm a girl from the big city and I only know about fashion and fabric and living out of a scrunched-up little apartment on the tough side of town?"

He twisted the bar stool so that he was facing her. As Lucinda took in his closeness, the broad width of his shoulders and the sensual curve to his lips, she felt the room shrink around them.

"No," he said to her question. "I figure most city people, from either side of the tracks, would like horses if they had the opportunity to be around them. I was talking about last night."

Lucinda's heart gave a couple of hard thuds against her breast then seemed to want to stop completely. "What about last night?" she asked, unaware that her voice had dipped to a cautious murmur.

His eyes met hers, lingered there, then dropped to her lips. Lucinda suddenly began to ache with the want to touch him, to have him kiss her again. The same way he'd kissed her last night.

"You were angry with me. I expected you to still be that way this morning."

She was surprised by his notion. Mainly because his thinking was so far from the truth. "I wasn't mad at you. If I recall, it was the other way around."

His expression rueful, he glanced down at his coffee mug. He didn't think he'd slept more than two hours last night. All he'd been able to think about was Lucinda and the way she'd looked when he'd told her he didn't share his private life with anyone. He'd hurt her. It had been all over her face. And though he'd never intended to do it, he couldn't forget that he'd caused her a moment's pain.

"I was a lot more angry with myself than I was with you. Hell, it's been so long since I've been around a woman for any length of time I—well, I guess I've gotten pretty rough around the edges."

"You live with two women," she pointed out.

He grimaced. "They're kin to me. You're different."

And she was making him different, Chance realized. Two days ago it wouldn't have mattered to him if he'd hurt Lucinda, or anyone who dared to bring up Jolene around him. He'd figured he had the right to lash out and protect his privacy. Losing Jolene and the baby had given him that right. But that was a crazy way of thinking. He could see that now and the revelation staggered him.

"I'm different? How do you mean?"

A wry smile twisted his lips. "I don't go around kissing my mother or sister—the way I kissed you."

Just having him mention the time she'd spent wound tightly in his arms set her heart to thumping. "Forget the kiss," she said huskily. "I already have."

Had she? Chance wondered. Then why didn't she look him in the eye instead of staring at the wall behind his head?

"How's your ankle?"

Relieved that he'd changed the subject, she stuck her foot out and showed him that her ankle had regained some of its former flexibility. "It's feeling better. It only pains a little to walk on it now."

"Then maybe you'll feel like walking through the horse barn after lunch. If I get things caught up, I'll come fetch you." He slid off the bar stool and carried his cup over to the kitchen sink. "Right now I'd better get to work. See you at breakfast."

See you at breakfast. The simple little phrase stayed with her as Chance left the room and she walked over to the plate glass door.

Yes, she would see him again at breakfast, she thought as she stared out at the early dawn sky, and she would be waiting for that time to come.

The admission frightened Lucinda. Sooner or later, she would have to head down the highway and get on with her life. She didn't want it to hurt when she left this place. She'd already dealt with enough pain in her life. She didn't think she could survive any more.

Later that morning, after learning the main highway was reasonably clear enough to travel, Dee and Sarah Jane headed to Hereford to do some last-minute Christmas shopping.

Lucinda declined their invitation to join them. Her ankle was better, but she didn't think it was quite up to that much exercise. Instead, she used the time to work on a pantsuit she'd started for Sarah Jane.

A few minutes before noon, the two women returned with a carful of presents. After everything was carried in, Dee began preparing lunch while Lucinda offered to help Sarah Jane wrap the gifts the two women had purchased this morning.

"How do you like these?" Sarah Jane asked Lucinda as they worked at the breakfast counter.

Lucinda looked at the earrings dangling from Sarah Jane's fingers. They were at least four inches long and made of pink, orange and red plastic beads. Lucinda figured whoever wore them had to be bold or crazy—or both.

"Well, they're—uh, bright," she said, trying her best to be polite and honest at the same time.

Across the room, Dee burst out laughing. "Lucy, you don't have to be so nice. They're the gaudiest things Sarah Jane could find."

"And believe me, I hunted hard," Sarah Jane said with a giggle.

"I'm almost afraid to ask who the earrings are for," Lucinda said, unable to keep from joining in on their laughter.

Sarah Jane carefully arranged the jewelry in a small box and fastened down the lid. "These are for Great-Aunt Bess. She'll love them."

"She's my aunt, on my mother's side," Dee spoke up. "She's a spry eighty-five and she loves dressing up. The wilder looking, the better."

"Sounds like a lady with fashion sense," Lucinda said.

Laughing, Sarah Jane handed the box to Lucinda. "Just wait until Christmas Day. You'll get to meet her then."

One by one the gifts were wrapped in bright foil paper and tagged with a name. A tie for one cousin and a bottle of Scotch for another, a box of candy for the closest neighbors and a furry stuffed kitten for their foster daughter. Each name had a story behind it and Lucinda enjoyed hearing Dee and Sarah Jane describe their friends and relatives. It made her feel a part of the family somehow.

"I wish you could have gone shopping with us this morning," Sarah Jane said as they worked their way through the gifts to be wrapped. "You might have found something you wanted to buy."

"Oh, I doubt it," Lucinda replied. "But I enjoy looking."

"Do you do much Christmas shopping?" Dee asked as she carried a bowl of salad to the table.

The question jerked Lucinda back to reality and the life she'd led back in Chicago. She'd never had the family and friends that the Delacroix had. But at one time she'd had a fairly large circle of friends and acquaintances. Yet Richard had changed that for her. Slowly and methodically, he'd cut her away from anyone close to her until finally her life had centered solely around him.

Now that Lucinda was away from him, it was easy to see that he'd been doing what nearly every abuser tried to do. Isolate the victim. Yet back then she'd been blinded to the fact of what he was doing to her life. She'd so desperately needed, wanted someone to love her that she'd ignored the first warning signals pointing to Richard's possessive behavior.

"I don't have much shopping to do," she answered Dee's question, unaware that Chance had walked into the room. "I gave my friends their gifts before I left Chicago."

"Don't you have distant family living somewhere in the States?"

Lucinda shook her head as she wound a red ribbon around the box in her hands. "No. My mother was killed in an accident when I was small and since I was placed in an orphanage I can only assume that she had no family."

"I told Lucinda she was lucky," Chance said as he walked up behind Lucinda and his sister. "She doesn't have to buy a lot of gifts. Like these."

With a curious smile on his face, he picked up a pair of red long johns and held them out in front of him.

"Those are for Doc," Dee spoke up before he could ask. "He's always telling me he's cold. I figure those will warm him up."

Laughing, Chance draped the underwear around his sister's neck. "Mother, he wants you to warm him up. Not a pair of long johns."

Dee snorted. "Well, he can stay cold till spring then."

"He wants to marry you, Mother," Sarah Jane pointed out.

"The old man doesn't know what he wants," Dee said with a wave of her hand. "He's got to convince me all that sweet talk of his is for real before he ever gets a yes out of me."

Lucinda glanced up from her task to see Chance grinning at his mother. After a moment, he looked at Lucinda and winked.

Why did he have to do that? she silently groaned as she jerked her eyes back on the ribbon she was tying. It made her feel flustered and even more foolish. Because for some reason, when Chance looked at her and winked, it made Lucinda believe she was special to him. And that kind of thinking was crazy. Lucinda Lambert wasn't special to anybody.

"Well, who's getting this for Christmas?" Chance asked, picking up a coiled lariat rope from the pile of gifts on the counter. "Me?"

"No. That's for Tim," Dee told him. Then to Lucinda, she said, "He's one of Chance's hired hands. Roping calves is his hobby."

In the flash of an eye, Chance built a loop then began twirling it about a foot or two off the floor.

"Chance! Quit!" Dee shouted at him.

Amazed, Lucinda watched as Chance jumped agilely inside the whirling loop, then back out again. She'd seen such a thing done in western movies before, but she'd believed it was probably done with a trick of the camera.

Waving a metal spatula, Dee ran at him. "Damn your hide, Chance, you're going to knock over my poinsettias! Now stop it!"

Laughing at his mother's scolding, he allowed the lariat rope to settle on the floor around his boots. As he coiled the braided nylon back together, he said, "I want Lucinda to know she's in West Texas, where the cowboys are real."

Sarah Jane groaned. "The cowboys are not only real, they love to show off, too."

Lucinda met his eyes and suddenly she was smiling at him. Whether he'd been showing off for her or not hardly mattered. She'd enjoyed seeing his playful antics.

"Can you do anything special with those other gifts?" Lucinda asked him, her smile turning impish.

He glanced at the pile of things the two women hadn't yet wrapped. "No. I'll leave those to you and Sarah Jane. Otherwise, Mother might send me out to the doghouse."

"No. I'm sending everyone to the table," Dee corrected her son. "Come on, girls, we'll finish all that wrapping later. It's time to eat."

After lunch, the three women finished the gift wrapping, then Lucinda went back to working on the designs for Sarah Jane's clothes. Normally she had plenty of time to allow her imagination to dwell upon certain styles and fabrics. But in this case, she only had a few days to complete her work. She was going to have to hurry in order to have everything ready to hand over to a seamstress before she left the ranch. Although Sarah Jane still had a few months before the wedding, Lucinda didn't want to mail anything back and leave a trail for someone to follow.

Even so, when Chance came for her later that afternoon, she didn't hesitate. She grabbed her coat and mittens and followed him outside.

The sun had steadily grown warmer throughout the day, and now melting snow dripped off the roof and left mushy puddles along the track leading down to the barns.

As the two of them stepped off the porch, Chance nodded toward a horse tied at the backyard gate.

"I brought taxi service," he told her.

Lucinda's mouth fell open as she looked at the horse, then her eyes swung back to Chance and she burst out laughing. "You can't expect me to ride a horse!"

"You don't want to strain your ankle by walking all the way down to the horse barn. And even though you don't weigh very much, Traveler can carry you a lot easier than I can."

Lucinda's gaze whipped from him to the sorrel horse standing quietly by the fence. He seemed docile enough. But she'd never been on a horse in her life!

"I know. But Chance, the closest I've ever been to a horse was in the grandstands at Maywood Park!"

Chance chuckled. "Well, Traveler is hardly a racehorse. He won't go anywhere unless I tell him to. And he's got one pace. Slow."

Lucinda wasn't a coward. But she knew if she didn't climb on Chance's horse, he would peg her as one. "Then I guess I'll put myself in your hands. Just remember I'm no Dale Evans."

"What? You mean you can't sing?" Chance joked as the two of them walked toward the horse.

She shot him a dry look. "No. I can't sing. Nor can I ride."

"Sure you can. Just because you've watched some old western movies on late-night TV, you think all horses rear straight up on their hind legs, whinny, then take off in a wild gallop. Believe me, Lucy, if they really did act that way, there wouldn't be any cowboys left. We'd all have broken necks."

"Well, now that I'm finally seeing you in the sunlight, yours does look a little bent," she said while studying him with exaggerated concern.

So Lucy did have a little humor in her, he thought, a smile tilting the corners of his roughly hewn lips. He liked that about her. But then Chance had to admit he was beginning to like quite a few things about her.

After untying Traveler's reins, Chance linked his fingers together and held them, palms up, near the stirrup.

"Give me your foot. The good one," he instructed. "And I'll help you into the saddle."

"If you insist." Taking a deep breath, Lucinda put the toe of her boot into his hands.

"I do insist. Now, when I lift, you grab hold of the horn and slide your leg over the saddle."

"What's the horn?" she asked frantically.

He patted a round thing wrapped with black rubber.

"Here we go," he warned, then gave her a boost upward.

Before Lucinda could figure out how she'd done it, she was sitting astride the big red horse. Chance quickly swung himself up behind her, then reined the horse away from the fence and toward the horse barn.

Lucinda was immediately swamped with sensations. The rhythm of the horse's walk rocked her gently from side to side and the ground looked to be a long way down. But it was Chance's nearness that was affecting her the most. His chest was brushing against her back and his thighs felt molded to the back of hers. If she turned her head slightly to the right, her forehead would bump into his chin. He didn't have to be that close, did he?

"Now what do you think about horseback riding?" he asked, his voice little more than a murmur in her ear. "Not nearly as scary as you thought it would be, is it?"

Lucinda wanted to groan as a shiver ran through her body. How could she think about the horse, or riding it, when he was touching her like this? "Oh, no. I'm not scared."

That much was the truth. She knew Chance could control the animal and he'd never allow her to fall. But riding a horse with a man who turned her senses haywire was not what she'd planned to do when she left Chicago.

"That's good. I like a woman who isn't afraid. I've tried for years to get Mother to ride. But she's terrified of horses. She's lived her life on this ranch for thirty-five years and never has been in the saddle. That's frustratin'. Real frustratin'."

I like a woman who isn't afraid. Well, he certainly wouldn't like her, Lucinda thought dismally. Not if he really knew her. If he knew how many nights she'd spent shaking in the darkness of her bedroom, afraid to close her eyes and sleep, he'd probably label her a helpless coward.

Maybe she was. Leaving Chicago certainly made her look that way. But she'd tried to confront Richard. She'd even tried getting help from the police. She'd personally gone down to the station to file a complaint. They had eyed the whole thing in a different light. To the police, she'd simply been an angry ex-fiancée out for revenge. Richard Winthrop was one of their own, a real asset to the homicide division, he would never stalk a woman!

Lucinda had come away from the whole thing looking foolish and even more embarrassed. After that, she'd never looked to the law for help. She'd realized it would be as useless as trying to climb a brick wall without any toeholds.

Chance pulled the horse up beside a long barn, slid off Traveler, then reached up to help Lucinda down. Seeing no other way to get to the ground, she placed her hands on his shoulders and allowed him to lift her from the saddle. As he set her to one side of him and the animal, Lucinda's hands slid off his shoulders and lingered on his forearms.

"Thanks," she murmured, her eyes carefully avoiding his.

"You're welcome, Lucy."

His quiet reply had her eyes darting up to his, and for a moment their gazes locked. Even with the coldness of the snowy ground all around them, Lucinda felt heat rise up within her, spread to her limbs and stain her cheeks with color. Something on his face, the strange light in his eyes told her that he hadn't forgotten the kiss they'd shared and he knew she was still thinking about it, too.

With one gloved forefinger, Chance reached out and touched her face. Lucinda trembled as the need to step closer to him argued with the sensible part of her that was screaming for her to move away.

"I don't think I've ever known a woman who blushes like you do."

"It's—my skin. It's very fair and sensitive to the cold," she said, hating the breathy sound of her voice.

Chance's dark eyebrows cocked up in speculation. "And here I was thinking I'd caused all that," he drawled.

Was he flirting with her? After the way he'd reacted to Jolene's name last night, it was hard to imagine Chance Delacroix flirting with any woman, much less Lucinda. There was nothing special about her. But he had kissed her, she mentally argued with herself. And that kiss had felt like a lot more than flirtation.

The whole, scary idea had her quickly turning away from him and looking at the barn. "Are you ready to show me the horses?"

No, Chance wasn't ready to show her the horses. He was thinking more on the line of taking her into his arms right then and there, just to prove to her that she wasn't as indifferent to him as she was trying to let on.

But that wouldn't be wise, he tried to tell himself. He hadn't brought her here for that reason. He'd invited her to the stables because she'd intimated an interest in the horses and he'd wanted to show off his herd to her. Hell, he'd gone for more than ten years without a woman in his life. Just because Lucinda was giving him certain urges didn't mean it was time to get another wife, or even a lover.

Besides, the argument in his head went on, Lucinda was a woman on the move. She was young and unsettled and she had her own career to think about. She wasn't his type of woman at all.

The reminder had him grabbing her upper arm and guiding her toward the barn. "Yeah, Lucy, I'm as ready as you are," he said.

But as they stepped through the door and Lucy's shoulder brushed against him, Chance wished like hell the hired hands hadn't gone into town for a load of feed. Without them around, he didn't know how he was going to keep his hands off her.

Chapter Seven

The first moment Lucinda stepped inside the huge structure, she noticed the pungent smell of alfalfa hay and the unfamiliar scent of horses. Sunlight slanted through the roof where sheets of corrugated iron had been replaced with a white, lighter weight material to create skylights at regular intervals.

Rows of stalls lined the back wall of the building, while to the front and the right of them was a closed-off room where, Lucinda guessed, feed and tack were stored. To the left of them were more empty stalls.

"The only time I keep all the horses in the barn is when the weather is as bad as it has been the past couple of days," Chance told her as he guided her over to the nearest group of animals.

"Where do they stay in summer?" she asked.

"In warm weather, all the horses are turned out to pastures. Except for the stud. He has to be separated from the rest for his own safety, as well as that of the herd."

She cast him a curious glance. "You raise horses, too?"

He nodded. "I've got about six or seven new foals coming this spring. Not a great amount. What we don't keep to use here on the ranch, I'll take to Clovis and sell."

As she and Chance approached the stall nearest to them, a tall black horse with a blazed face hung his head over the metal gate that served as a door.

Chance gave the animal's jaw an affectionate pat. "This is Big John. He's one of the smartest cow ponies here on the ranch. I wouldn't sell him for any amount of money."

"What is a cow pony? He looks a lot bigger than a pony to me," Lucinda said, carefully standing a good two feet away from Big John's head.

Chance chuckled and Lucinda shot him a defensive look. "Obviously my ignorance about ranch life amuses you."

Frowning, he shook his head. "I don't think you're ignorant about anything. I'd be just as lost if you showed me a dress pattern. As for your question about the cow pony, that's just a term we cowboys use for a horse or mare that can be used on a ranch to head or cut cattle from another herd. Or if need be, we can rope off them."

Lucinda's chin lifted a fraction higher. "Well, something is making you laugh."

Chance grabbed hold of her hand and pulled her toward him and the horse. "I'm laughing because you're standing back there like Big John is going to take a bite out of you."

"How do you know he won't?"

Before Lucinda could protest, Chance took her hand and placed it on the horse's face. "This horse wouldn't bite a fly. Unless that fly was biting him. Go ahead, give him a good pat. He loves it."

Cautiously at first, Lucinda stroked her hand down the horse's nose. Big John didn't bare his teeth at her, so she rubbed his face again. However, the moment she drew her hand away, the horse nudged her shoulder.

"Is he trying to tell me to keep petting him?" Lucinda asked with surprise.

"Sure he is," Chance answered. "Most horses are very affectionate. They'll follow you around like a dog."

"I didn't realize that," Lucinda admitted, moving closer to the horse. "But then I don't know anything about horses. Or dogs, either, for that matter. Except for the strays I encountered on the city streets."

"You never had a pet? Or you just don't like animals?"

With a shake of her head, Lucinda said, "We didn't have pets in the orphanage. I guess there were already too many human mouths to feed. After I was out on my own, I moved to an apartment where pets weren't allowed." She shrugged one slender shoulder. "I always thought it would be cruel, anyway, to house an animal up all day by itself while I was away at work."

"Having four thousand acres, it's hard to imagine not having a yard big enough for a dog to run in."

"I'm sure it is. But to me, having four thousand acres to care for would be mind-boggling."

Chance guided her to the next stall. As they walked, he said, "It's a challenge. But I wouldn't want to do anything else. I guess raising cattle and horses is in my blood. My grandfather first started the D Bar D. Dad took over after he died. Now it's gone to me."

Even through the material of her coat, Chance's arm against the back of her waist felt warm. Lucinda tried to tell herself she didn't like it, that she wished he'd quit touching her altogether. But she knew she'd only be lying to herself. Having him walk beside her like this made her feel secure. Something she hadn't felt in a long, long time.

"You don't ever feel like the ranch is too much for you?"

The two of them paused at the next stall long enough for Lucinda to see a sorrel mare bedded down in the loose wood shavings covering the floor.

"The ranch has never been too much for me," Chance said as he guided her down the alleyway. "But I have to admit that it's sometimes been a little rough trying to take care of Mother and Sarah Jane. Especially after Dad died. They both turned to me and there wasn't any way I could take the place of a husband and father."

"It must have been an awful time for all of you."

He sighed. "It was. Mother was desperately depressed and nothing I did seemed to help bring her out of it. Sarah Jane was just a fourth grader, who thought her big brother could work miracles and bring her father back. I'm sure I let both of them down back then."

Lucinda couldn't imagine a man like Chance thinking he'd let anyone down. He seemed so strong, so sure of himself and his family. "As long as you stayed here on the ranch and tried to help them, then you couldn't have let them down."

Chance didn't agree. He'd always felt as though he'd let everyone down. Especially Jolene and his unborn daughter. She'd loved him, expected and depended on him to take care of her. Instead, he'd let her die giving birth to his child. The wound of that went so deep inside him, he doubted a lifetime would heal it.

His hand slipped away from her shoulder and Lucinda knew he'd set himself apart from her now. He was back in his own private thoughts. A place where she wasn't welcome. And though Lucinda tried to ignore it, a cold, deserted feeling began to seep through her.

Needing to change the subject, he said, "Come on. There's a little fellow down here that I think you'll like to see."

The fellow turned out to be a colt. His white coat was splotched with bay red spots and his unruly mane stuck out all directions. The moment he saw Chance and Lucinda he nickered and trotted over to them.

"He was born in May, so he's nearly eight months now. You like him?"

Just when she was telling herself that Chance was a stranger and she wanted him to stay that way, he had to go and smile at her as if she were somebody special to him. Why did he have to torment her like that?

"He's adorable. What's his name?"

"I haven't registered a formal name for him yet. I'm going to let Sarah Jane do that. She doesn't know it, but this little guy is going to be her wedding present from me."

She turned her head to look at him. "She can ride?"

Chance chuckled. "Don't let her know it, but Sarah Jane can outride me any day."

Lucinda had always believed gray was a cool, somber color. In fact, she rarely used it in her designs. But as she looked into Chance's gray eyes, she realized they were anything but cool. They were warm and inviting and quickly dissolving her last bit of common sense.

"You must love her a lot," Lucinda said quietly.

The expression on Lucinda's face was like that of a lost little girl, Chance thought. One that was always peering into the window and wondering what it was like to live like the rest of the world. And suddenly he wanted more than anything to wipe that look away. He wanted to draw her to him. Not just because it would feel good to have her soft body pressed to his. No, he wanted to show her, tell her that she wasn't alone and unloved. Dear God, what was happening to him? he wondered.

"She's my sister. I want her to be happy."

Even though I can't be. Chance hadn't spoken the words, but Lucinda had heard them just the same. She suddenly yearned to ask him about Jolene. Why couldn't he let go of her memory and give himself a chance to find happiness with someone else?

But Lucinda kept the questions to herself. Chance's life, or what he did with it, wasn't her business. She was just a temporary guest and she knew that Chance wouldn't hesitate to remind her of the fact.

In silent agreement, they moved on through the barn, lingering long enough at each stall for Chance to introduce its occupant to Lucinda. Eventually her ankle began to ache and she told Chance she'd better go back to the house.

"There's one more thing I want to show you before we go," he said.

Curious, she followed him through a door and into a dark room. Chance pulled a string hanging from the ceiling and a light bulb glared to life. Blinking from the sudden light, she glanced around her.

Covered barrels lined one wall, while the back end of the room was stacked several feet deep with feed sacks. Saddles, some new looking and some old and worn, hung by their horns from ropes thrown over the rafters. The sweet smell of molasses mixed with the scent of leather and saddle soap filled the room.

Intrigued by the unfamiliar sights and smells, Lucinda stood in the middle of the room and drank it all in. "Is this what you wanted to show me? What do you call this? A feed room? A tack room?"

Chance smiled as he watched her eyes roam over an intricately carved fender on a saddle. Her curiosity pleased him, because each saddle and horse were like old, familiar friends to him. He wanted her to like them as much as he did.

"Actually, it's a little bit of both. But the room isn't what I wanted to show you. Come here."

She wound her way through the saddles to where he squatted near a pile of empty feed sacks. Behind them, curled up on an old saddle blanket was a brindle-colored mother cat with four kittens.

"Oh, how precious!" Lucinda exclaimed with undisguised pleasure.

Kneeling down beside Chance, she leaned over for a better look. "Will the mother let you touch them?"

"Sure. She's an old hand around here. She knows we won't hurt her babies." To prove it, he reached over and scratched mother cat between the ears, then picked up one of the kittens. It was a yellow-striped tabby with four white feet.

"Here," he said, handing the kitten to Lucinda. "Hold him and see how you like him."

Even though she knew it was probably childish, she couldn't help oohing and aahing over the furry little animal.

"He's beautiful," Lucinda murmured. "I'm sure he'll look very regal when he grows up."

She was cuddling the ball of fur to her cheeks as if he were more precious than a diamond. And the sight touched a place inside Chance that he hadn't even known existed before now.

"I want you to have him," he told her.

Lucinda lifted her eyes to Chance. His face was only inches away, so near she could see the pores in his skin, the faint ragged line of his bottom lip, the warm light in his eyes. And in that moment she felt very close to him, closer than she'd ever felt to anyone in her life.

"You want me to have him?" she asked, unaware that her voice had dropped to an awed whisper.

She made it sound as if he were giving her the world, and for the first time in a long time, Chance felt a sense of pure joy fill his chest and spread a smile across his face.

"Yeah. I want him to be yours. Don't you like him?"

She glanced down at the kitten cradled gently in her palms, then back to Chance. "I love him. But Chance, what would I do with a cat? I'm headed to California."

Suddenly some of the pleasure of his gift faded. "Well, surely cats live in California, too," he reasoned.

"I'm sure they do. But I'll probably be in a city. I might not have a yard, or a place for him to roam."

His eyes studied her face. "That's important to you, isn't it? That living things have enough space to roam free."

Suddenly Lucinda was back in the orphanage in the long drab room she shared with several other girls. After several years passed, it had become a cage to her. "When I lived in the orphanage," she said quietly, "I used to wish I were a bird so I could fly free, go anywhere I wanted. I wouldn't have people telling me when to go to bed, or wake up, when I could or couldn't eat."

A wry slant to his mouth, he said, "Most kids resent being told what to do, no matter where they live."

"You're right. But living by such a strict schedule made me yearn for my independence. When I was finally old enough to get it, I cherished it. Then Richard, my ex-fiancé, he came along and—"

She broke off abruptly, amazed that she'd been about to open up that private part of her life to him.

"And what?" he urged.

With her forefinger, Lucinda stroked the little yellow tom between the ears. "Richard did his best to take away my hard-earned independence. He wanted to control everything I did and said. Right down to who I could have for friends. Even the color of my clothes. I couldn't bear it. No matter where I am, or whomever I'm with, I have to be me. Just me."

Reaching over, Chance gently touched her arm. "I have a feeling this little guy will understand. He'll give you your space and you can give him his."

Lucinda tried to swallow down the lump of emotion filling her throat. "I just don't want his space to be city concrete. It wouldn't be fair."

His eyebrows lifted with speculation. "Maybe it wouldn't have to be. Maybe you could live somewhere else."

Why did she suddenly get the feeling he was talking about more than this little kitten's future home? "I suppose it's possible. I guess it isn't written in stone that I have to live in a city. But where my work is concerned, it would make things easier."

A brief smile touched his face. "Well, whatever you decide about that, I'm sure you'll give this little guy a good home."

"You really do want me to have him, don't you?" she asked again, as though she still couldn't quite believe it.

"I do. He's my Christmas gift to you."

Lucinda knew she'd never received anything that meant more to her. She didn't know why. Pets were given all the time as gifts. And if she'd really wanted a kitten that badly she could have purchased one at a pet store. But this was different. This kitten represented more than a pet. He was the idea that she really could have a better life. And Chance had given it to her.

Gently she placed the kitten down with the other three, who were wrestling playfully beside their mother. "I'll leave him with his family until I'm ready to go," she told Chance, then smiled. "I think I'll call him Caesar. He has a noble-looking nose."

Chuckling, Chance rose to his feet and pulled Lucinda along with him. "All tomcats have big noses. But you don't have to tell Caesar that."

Before she could stop herself, Lucinda reached up and laid her palm against his cheek. It felt warm and stubby with whiskers, and incredibly precious to her.

"Thank you, Chance. You're a generous man."

No. He wasn't generous, Chance thought. He was selfish. Years ago he'd wanted Jolene, and because he had, she'd died. Now he was wanting Lucinda the same way and he knew that whatever she did or said, he couldn't give in to those wants. Not if he really cared about her. And he did care about her. The realization of it was becoming stronger and stronger, no matter how he tried to deny it.

"You're welcome," he said huskily, then clearing his throat, he pulled her hand down and led her out of the feed room. "We'd better get back to the house. It's cold in here and you've been on your ankle too long."

As they left the horse barn, Lucinda knew the tender moment they'd shared was gone forever. But she would always remember it in her heart and no one could take that away from her.

When Chance reined in Traveler back at the ranch house, Lucinda's car was parked near the fence. Pulled up next to it was a white patrol car with the word *sheriff* written across it.

Fear rushed through Lucinda, turning her blood to ice water. What was the law doing here? she wondered frantically. Had Richard somehow tracked her down through his network of police friends? Dear God, if he had, all the miles she'd fled would be in vain. Her chance for peace and happiness would be gone.

Chance had just helped her down from the horse when a tall, dark-haired man strolled out of the house and on to the back porch. He was wearing a khaki uniform with a pistol belted at his hip. The shiny badge pinned to his shirt pocket signified his authority.

"Well, hello, Chance. Is all this sunshine agreeing with you?"

Lucinda stood immobilized as she stared at the Texas lawman. On the other hand, Chance seemed glad to see him. Taking her by the arm, he led her toward the house and the waiting sheriff.

"I could use several more days like this," Chance told him. "What brings you out here today?"

"Just wanted to say hey to everybody. I ran into Mike down on the highway. He said he'd been instructed to bring this car up here to the ranch." He motioned with his head toward Lucinda's car.

"That's right," Chance told him. "It belongs to Miss Lambert here. She's staying on the ranch with us for a few days."

The sheriff tipped his cream-colored Stetson at her. "Nice to meet you, ma'am."

Lucinda could scarcely breathe. "Are you here to give me a driving ticket?" she asked him.

Chance immediately burst out laughing. As soon as he did, the young sheriff smiled at her. Totally confused by their behavior, Lucinda glanced frantically from one man to the other.

"No, ma'am. I figure your sliding off in the ditch was due to Mother Nature and not your driving. I just like to check in on my cousin every few days and make sure he's not getting into trouble."

Surprised, she looked from one man to the other. "You two are cousins?"

"On my Dad's side," Chance told her. "So there are two Delacroix men in this county."

"Yeah, and Chance is the ugly one."

Lucinda was beginning to see the resemblance between them now. She was also trembling with relief. Apparently Richard hadn't sent him looking for a Lucinda Lambert from Chicago.

"Yeah, but it's obvious that I got the brains," Chance told him.

The sheriff, who looked to be around the same age as Chance, laughed and clapped his cousin on the back.

"Are you going to be here for Christmas, Miss Lambert?"

She nodded at him hesitantly. "I think so."

"Then you're in for a big treat. Aunt Dee's the best cook this side of the Pecos."

"Too bad you'll have to miss it," Chance spoke up.

He shot Chance a mocking glance. "That's what you think. I just gave her a pheasant to bake for Christmas dinner."

"We're having turkey."

"I'm having pheasant, too," he told Chance, then laughing, he climbed into the patrol car. "You two behave. That's an order."

With a good-natured groan, Chance waved him out of the driveway. "That boy is—" Chance's words came to an abrupt halt as he turned around to see Lucinda limping hurriedly toward the house. "Lucinda?"

She didn't answer or acknowledge that she'd heard him. Cursing under his breath, he trotted after her. Just as she was about to step up onto the porch, he caught her by the arm.

"What's the matter? Are you in that big of a hurry to get away from me?"

Lucinda darted a glance at him, then as quickly looked away. "I'm—just cold."

She looked more than cold to Chance. Her face was as white as the snow on the ground and she was trembling so badly her teeth were chattering. "You look like you've seen a ghost! What's frightened you?"

Frustrated with herself and with him, she tried to shake the hold he had on her arm, but her efforts only made him tighten his grip.

"There's nothing wrong with me," she said, trying her best to sound convincing.

"I see. That's why you're quaking like a leaf. That's why you were running to the house. Are you trying to completely ruin your ankle?"

Something about the tone of his voice struck a nerve inside Lucinda, making resentment flare in her eyes as she glared up at him. "If you really must know, your cousin scared me. So there! Can you quit questioning me now? Because I don't like it!"

His brows shot up, then pulled into a disbelieving line above his eyes. How could she be scared of Troy? And why was she suddenly so defensive? This wasn't the woman he was talking to a few minutes ago in the barn.

"Troy scared you? That's crazy!"

Gritting her teeth, she jerked her arm free of his grasp. "Then I guess I'm crazy!"

Not waiting around to be badgered with more questions, she ran into the house. Dee was at the kitchen sink, but Lucinda hurried on past Chance's mother and down the hall to her bedroom.

Once inside with the door shut, she tore off her coat and sank onto the edge of the bed. Her hands were shaking and her cheeks, which had been ice-cold a few moments ago were now flaming with heat.

Pressing her palms to her face, she groaned out loud. What was the matter with her? She'd gotten upset over nothing. Now Chance was going to think she was crazy or worse!

But the fear that Richard might have tracked her down and sent the sheriff after her had been so great she'd been frozen with it. By the time she'd learned differently, aftershock had taken over.

"Lucy!"

Chance's roar was followed by a knock on the bedroom door. Before Lucinda could yell at him to go away, he strode into the room as if he owned it.

Lucinda jumped up from the bed. "What do you want?"

"I wasn't through with you," he said angrily.

The authoritative tone of his words infuriated Lucinda. Richard had treated her as if he owned her. He considered her to be his object to be questioned, insulted or discarded whenever he chose. She'd be damned to hell before she'd allow another man to treat her that way.

"Well, I was certainly through with you," she retorted, then swiping her tousled hair away from her face, she turned and walked over to the armchair where she'd left her sketch pad. "Now I'd like to get back to work. If you don't mind," she added coldly.

Chance didn't understand her anger or where it was coming from. At least, he thought with some relief, it had brought some color back to her face. A few moments ago, she'd been so pale he'd fully expected her to keel over in a dead faint.

"I do mind," Chance told her. "I'd like to know why Troy set off such a scare in you. He wasn't about to give you a ticket or anything like—"

Whirling back around to him, Lucinda clutched the sketch pad to her breast. "I wasn't worried about a ticket!

I just don't like policemen. They—" She glanced away from his searching eyes. "They frighten me," she finished, her voice suddenly quiet and resigned.

"Frighten you?" He echoed her question as though he weren't certain he'd heard her right. "That doesn't make sense. If you can't trust a policeman, you're living in a pretty scary place."

Lucinda *had* been living in a scary place. But Chance would never understand if she tried to explain about Richard. From what he'd just said, it was obvious he was like all the rest, she thought wearily. Richard would never harm her, he was a trusted law official. Was everyone blind, or was it she who wasn't capable of seeing things clearly?

Chance didn't know what to think as he watched an array of emotions race across Lucinda's face. There was sadness and resignation. But more than that, the look on her face said she was hiding something. Something that she didn't want him or anyone to know about.

"Lucy?" he began quietly. "Did you leave Chicago because you were in trouble with the law?"

The fixed stare of her gaze suddenly jerked off the floor and up at him. Outrage widened her eyes and made her bottom lip quiver. "You think—I've broken the law? You think I'm a thief or a murderer, or—"

Stepping forward, Chance grabbed her by the shoulders. "You see a sheriff and you nearly collapse with fright. What am I supposed to think?"

She'd only known this man for little more than two days. It shouldn't matter if he thought she was a fugitive, or worse. But it did. It cut her to the very bone. Less than an hour ago in the barn, she'd thought that he actually cared for her, that he believed in her as a person. God, how wrong could she have been!

Hopeless tears burned her eyes and threatened to spill over onto her cheeks. Desperate to hide them from him, she twisted her head away and squeezed her eyes tightly shut. "I guess you can think whatever you want to think," she said, her voice wobbling around the lump in her throat.

"That's all you have to say?"

"What do you want me to say?" she asked, defeat pouring through her, settling around her heart like a ring of cold rock. "Do you want me to tell you all about myself? What good would that do? You wouldn't believe half of what I told you. And even if you would, I don't want to tell you. Just like you don't want to tell me about Jolene."

Anger swiftly set Chance's jaw like a piece of concrete. "Why do you keep bringing Jolene into things? You think because I've lost my wife that I've lost my manhood, too?"

Lucinda didn't know where his thinking was coming from, but if he wanted to be insulting, she could, too. Raking a glare up and down his tall, muscular body, she said, "It's obvious you lost your heart. As for your manhood, I'm not in any position to say."

The words were hardly past her lips before he yanked her up against him. "I can remedy that for you. Right now!"

Before Lucinda could jerk away, his thumb and forefinger caught her chin and held it fast. She stared defiantly up at him. "You don't want to kiss me, Chance! You think I'm a felon. Or—or something equally bad."

His mouth twisted into a mocking sneer. "Oh, you're bad all right, Lucy. Very bad for me."

"And you're—"

Lucinda didn't go on. She couldn't. Suddenly his mouth was on hers, hard, hot and demanding. She squirmed against him and tried to wedge her hands between her and his broad chest, but he was holding her so tightly she doubted a piece of thread would slide between them.

Seconds later, it didn't matter. The pressure of his lips softened and the tight grip he had on her waist eased. His hands took a slow, spiraling path up her back until his fingers finally reached her hair. Once they did, they threaded themselves into the silky strands, pressed against her scalp and begged her to answer his hungry lips.

Lucinda didn't disappoint him. With a soft groan, her lips parted beneath his and her hands slid across his shoulders, then gripped the back of his neck.

Kissing Chance was like stepping into a warm, mysterious cave. She knew it was dangerous to continue onward, but she wanted to see, to feel what the next step would bring. And when his tongue invaded her mouth, she savored its taste and texture, reveled in the heat that was pooling in the center of her body.

Lucinda wanted to make love to him. It was that simple. She wanted to give her body to a man who doubted her character. A man whose heart was buried with another woman.

That last thought was enough to give Lucinda the strength to tear her lips away from his. "I can't—don't do this to me," she pleaded, twisting her head to one side and gulping in a deep breath.

Chance released his hold on her, then slowly took a step back. He didn't know how things between them had escalated to this point. But one thing was for sure, he didn't want the passion to end. He wanted to lift her off her feet, pitch her backward onto the bed and see her arms reach out to him. He wanted to see a look of love in her eyes and know that it was only for him.

As he studied her bent head, her slumped shoulders, her trembling hands, he wondered if he'd gone crazy. He didn't know this woman! And from what she'd just told him, she didn't want him to know her.

"I wasn't doing anything to you that you didn't want," he said finally, his voice low and rough.

Lucinda's head whipped around to him. "Well, I'll not want it again! I may not have much in this world, Chance Delacroix, but I do have my pride and my independence. I won't let you take those away. Not you or any man!"

Did she honestly think that's what he wanted from her? And why would she? Shaking his head in confusion, Chance stepped toward her. "Lucy, you're crazy if you think—"

"Yes, I'm crazy all right," she furiously interrupted him. "Damn crazy for thinking you might be different!"

"Different from what? Who?"

She looked at him, opened her mouth to answer, then just as quickly closed it. She wasn't going to argue with him. She wasn't going to look at him, and most of all she wasn't going to want him. She was going to put an end to everything here and now. It was the smartest, safest thing she could do.

Her lips compressed in a tight line, she pointed toward the door. "Get out!"

Chance couldn't ever remember a woman shouting at him. Nor could he think of a time he'd ever been more furious.

"Gladly," he yelled back at her, then turned and slammed out of the room.

Chapter Eight

After the windows quit rattling and she was certain he wasn't coming back, Lucinda walked on shaky legs to the closet and quickly pulled out her suitcases. She couldn't stay here now. The mere idea that Chance believed she was a—a what? she asked herself. He hadn't accused her of doing or being one certain thing. But he'd certainly doubted her innocence and that was enough to convince Lucinda it was time to leave. That and her melting all over him as if he were her long-lost lover.

What had she been thinking? Why had she goaded him like that about Jolene? It was clear that he didn't want to share anything personal with her. But that hadn't stopped her from wanting him to. Nor had it stopped her from wanting to kiss him. So she'd taunted him.

Well, she'd had her foolish, reckless moment with him and now it was over. Now it was time to get back to the real world where she belonged. Chance, his mother and his sister were beginning to matter to her, she realized, and that was a mistake. She couldn't let herself get attached to people. Attachments only meant pain further down the line.

She was tossing undergarments into a suitcase when the bedroom door suddenly flew open and Dee burst into the room.

"Lucy! What in the world is going on? I could hear you and Chance shouting all the way down to the kitchen. Now he's slammed out of the house in a black temper."

Keeping her head bent, Lucinda wiped frantically at the tears on her face. She'd never been a crier. She'd learned long ago it was useless to shed tears. But this time they continued to pour down her face in spite of her determination to stop them.

"Chance and I—had a disagreement," she said to Dee. "I'm sorry if I've upset you."

"Upset me?" Dee asked, incredulous that Lucinda was putting her feelings first. "Don't worry about me. I want to know what my son has done to you. Why are you crying? And why are you packing?"

Lucinda swallowed, then said, "I can't stay here any longer, Dee. It would be too uncomfortable for me and your son."

Her forehead puckered with concern, Dee studied Lucinda's tear-blotched face. "But why? Did my son make a pass at you?"

Lucinda groaned miserably. Dear Lord, what would Dee think if she knew just how far things had gone between her and her son? She would probably think Lucinda was just a gold digger, roaming across the country in search of a gullible man. Chance certainly believed she was a no-good.

Rising up from the suitcase, Lucinda wiped her cheeks with the backs of her hands. "It's nothing like that—"

"Well, it should've been!" Dee swiftly interrupted. "My son needs his head turned by a woman. I thought you'd be pretty enough to do it."

Surprised and touched by Dee's words, Lucinda shook her head. "Pretty isn't enough to turn Chance's head. I'm afraid your son is a closed book, Dee. I pity any woman who tries to read him."

Moving closer, Dee placed her hand on Lucinda's shoulder and gave it a reassuring squeeze. "Then what were you two going on about? Surely it wasn't important enough to make you leave."

Drawing in a shaky breath, Lucinda closed her burning eyes. It wasn't right to shut Dee out. The woman had been too kind to her. She deserved some sort of explanation. "Chance believes I left Chicago because—well, because I did something wrong and I'm running from the law."

For a moment there was dead silence. Lucinda opened her eyes just in time to see Dee tilting her head back and roaring with laughter.

"Oh, my!" she said after a moment. "That's a good one. I didn't realize my son had such a wild imagination."

Lucinda looked at her skeptically. "You don't believe him?"

Dee began laughing again. "Of course not! Chance is a good judge of horseflesh, but people?" Shaking her head, she tapped her chest with her forefinger. "I'm the one who knows people. And I knew the moment I looked at you that you were someone I'd be proud to know."

"But Chance—"

Dee interrupted with a wave of her hand. "Chance is—I wouldn't say he's a suspicious person. But he is very cautious. I guess that comes from losing Jolene and—well, it's made him overprotective, I think."

Lucinda was still trying to digest the older woman's words when Dee reached around her and flipped over the half-packed suitcase.

"You put all those things back where they belong and forget about Chance."

"But he—" Lucinda tried again, only to have Dee quickly intervene with a firm shake of her head.

"If Chance questioned you, Lucy, it's because deep down he wants to know you better. And subtlety never was one of my son's virtues." She patted Lucinda's cheek, then started toward the door. "Now dry those tears," she tossed over her shoulder. "I don't allow crying in the Delacroix house at Christmastime."

Atop a gentle rise, Chance reined Traveler to a stop and slowly scanned the snow-laden plains. He didn't know where the hell that cow was. Back at the feed troughs, he'd counted forty-nine head. Three times. In this particular pasture there were supposed to be fifty head. None of which were due to calve for at least two more months.

Muttering a curse under his breath, he turned the horse back toward the feeding grounds and jammed his gloved hands into the pockets of his coat.

The sun was rapidly falling and the temperature along with it. He'd been riding for at least two hours now and his feet had long ago gone numb from the cold. There was no use in staying out longer, he realized. Soon it would be too dark to see his way home, much less find a downed cow. When he got back to the house, he'd call his neighbor, Jim Freeman. If Chance was lucky, she'd gotten through the fence somehow and had taken up with his holsteins.

It took thirty more minutes for Chance to ride his way back to the feeding grounds. The herd of black Angus was still there, feeding on several round bales of hay that he and Tim had hauled out here earlier in the day.

Should he count again? Maybe she had walked in from the west side of the pasture while he'd been searching the east side. Deciding to give it one last try, Chance reined his mount to a stop several yards away from the milling herd and quickly began to count in twos.

Fifty! He counted again. Then again. All fifty cows were there and from what Chance could see in the falling twilight, they all looked healthy. Had he simply miscounted earlier?

Hell, it wouldn't surprise him if he had, he thought as he nudged Traveler into a fast walk. He hadn't been thinking straight at all since Lucinda had arrived on the ranch. And after this afternoon, he wasn't able to think, period.

That's what a woman did to a man, Chance mused as he miserably ducked his face against the cold north wind. It wasn't enough for a woman to tie a man's body into frustrated knots. No, they had to go for the heart and the mind, too. Right now Chance didn't know which of the three was giving him the most problems. Worse than that, he didn't know how to fix any of them.

"Chance, I was about to get on a horse and come looking for you myself!" Dee scolded him, when more than a half hour later he walked into the kitchen. "It's been dark for ages!"

Leaning down, Chance kissed his mother's cheek, then tiredly pulled off his hat. "If I'd known you were about to get up enough nerve to ride, I'd have stayed out later."

Shaking her head at him, she hurried over to the stove where she was frying pork steak in a huge iron skillet. "Where have you been anyway? The hands have been gone for at least an hour or more."

"A cow was missing over in the east pasture. I was looking for her."

Dee glanced up from the frying meat to see her son swipe a weary hand over his face. "Did you find her?"

He nodded. "Finally. Is supper ready?"

"By the time you wash, it will be," Dee told him.

Down the hallway, in his bedroom, Chance sluiced his face with hot water, cleaned his hands, then changed his muddy denim shirt for a plaid flannel. His jeans were also muddy and splotched with manure, but he didn't have time to change them or his boots. He'd do that later when he got ready for bed. And the way he felt at the moment, that wouldn't be too long from now.

"Tea or coffee, Chance?" Sarah Jane asked as he took a seat at the dining table.

"Coffee. I need something to unthaw me."

She poured him a cup and passed it down to him. Dee joined them at the table with a platter of biscuits.

Chance glanced from his mother and sister, then to Lucinda's empty chair. When he'd passed her bedroom in the hallway, he'd noticed a light coming from under the door, but he'd figured she'd simply left it on.

"Lucinda isn't coming to eat?" Dee asked Sarah Jane.

Sarah Jane shook her head glumly, then slanted an accusing look at her brother.

"No. She said she wasn't hungry."

"The child has to be hungry," Dee reasoned with a frown. "She didn't eat but a few bites at lunch."

"I tried my best," Sarah Jane said. "She doesn't want to join us. She says she wants to finish that pantsuit pattern she's been working on all evening."

Dee held the platter of biscuits out to Chance. He forked three to his plate before passing them on to his sister.

"There isn't any need for her to finish each one of those designs before she leaves here," Dee told Sarah Jane. "Your wedding isn't until May. She can mail the patterns back to us, if need be."

"I'm going to tell her that," Sarah Jane said with a nod of her head. "And I'll take her a tray of something later. Maybe she'll eat then."

Chance suddenly slammed down his fork. "What the hell are you going to do that for? She doesn't need to be coddled!"

Sarah Jane turned a glare on her brother. "No. She needs to be treated like a human being. Something, it appears, that you've forgotten how to do."

Chance frowned at her. "What's that supposed to mean? It isn't my fault that Lucy doesn't want to come out and face us!"

"And just whose fault is it, Chance? Mother and I weren't the ones who accused her of being a fugitive from the law!"

"She told you that?"

He was close to shouting the question. Dee looked at him calmly. "I had a talk with Lucy, Chance."

"And now I'm supposed to feel guilty because I questioned her about leaving Chicago? That shouldn't have insulted her. Unless she's guilty of something."

Sarah Jane made a snorting noise while Dee said, "Perhaps it was the way you went at it?"

Chance's eyes lifted to the ceiling. "She's supposed to be handled with kid gloves. Is that what you're trying to say?"

"I'm just saying you could be a little more sensitive," Dee suggested.

Frowning, Chance stabbed a biscuit with his fork, then ripped it open. "Why should I be? The woman pumps me for private information."

Sarah Jane groaned. "Chance, it's a good thing you've never been inclined to marry again. The way you are, I doubt you'd have much luck keeping a wife."

A cold, distant look crept slowly over his features. "I doubt I would, either. After all, I didn't with the first one, did I?"

Sarah Jane's expression was suddenly remorseful. "Oh, I—I'm sorry, Chance. I didn't mean it like that. I wasn't talking about Jolene."

Chance was suddenly too weary to eat. Picking up his coffee cup, he rose to his feet. "Forget it, sis."

Tears welled in Sarah Jane's eyes. "I'm sorry, brother," she said quietly.

Stepping around to her chair, Chance bent down and kissed her cheek. "Don't be sorry. Forget it and eat your supper before James throws you over for a woman with some meat on her bones."

At the far end of the house, there was a study that Chance used as an office. He hated paperwork and usually put it off until his desk was running over with statements and receipts. But tonight he was looking for anything to get his mind off Lucinda.

In the small room, he switched on a desk lamp, then turned on the radio. The Amarillo station, which normally played country music, was now into the Christmas season. Brenda Lee was belting out "Jingle Bell Rock."

On the right-hand corner of the desk, feed bills were stacked elbow high. One by one Chance began posting them in the ledger. As he came to the last and latest one, he growled a curse word under his breath.

Horse feed had taken a sharp rise. Twenty cents a sack. With his ink pen, he scratched out a quick tabulation on the margin of the ledger book. At that rate, he'd be paying eighty dollars more a ton. Three hundred and forty dollars more a month.

Tossing the bill to one side, he leaned back in his chair and linked his hands at the back of his neck. The ranch could absorb the extra expense, but he'd definitely rather be spending the money for new fencing.

Chance supposed he could get rid of two, maybe three of the older horses, but in the long run that wouldn't save the ranch all that much money. Besides, he might as well face it, he was attached to all of them, and deciding which two or three to sell, would be like deciding which leg or arm he wanted to give up. That's why he'd been eager to show the horses to Lucinda. They were like his children and he'd wanted her to enjoy them as much as he did.

Lucinda! Why did she keep coming back to his thoughts? Why couldn't he forget about the way he'd kissed her? The way she'd kissed him back!

A knock on the door interrupted his thoughts. Knowing how his mother hated it when a person didn't eat, he expected to see her come waltzing into the room with a loaded tray of food.

Without looking around, he said, "Mother, I'm not starving to death, I'll eat—"

"It's not your mother."

Chance's head whipped around, then his breath drew in sharply as he saw Lucinda standing just inside the door.

"Lucy."

No man had ever said her name that way, with his voice somehow both soft and rough, so full of emotion. The sweetness of the sound lifted her eyes to his face and for long moments she simply looked at him.

"I—don't want to disturb you," she said, then nervously licking her lips, she took one step closer.

She'd already disturbed the hell out of him. And he'd already decided that she was going to stay in his head whether she was in this room with him, or some other part of the house.

"You're not disturbing me. Come in."

Reaching behind her, she gently pushed the door shut, then clasped her hands in front of her. The room was small and dimly lit. One small lamp burned on the desk. Its light pooled on the pages of the open ledger and reflected up to Chance's face. She could see that his gray eyes were red with fatigue while black whiskers shadowed his chin and jaws and upper lip. She'd thought about him all evening, the things she'd said to him and the way she'd felt in his arms. Now that she was standing here looking at him, all she could think about was going to him and laying her cheek against his.

"Was there something you wanted?" he asked.

Dear God, yes. She wanted him. Couldn't he see it all over her face? Each time she looked at him, even thought of him, a surge of yearning poured through her like kerosene on fire. And she seemed powerless to stop it.

Taking another step closer, she said, "Yes. I—I've been thinking about—" She breathed in deeply and tried again. "The way I behaved this afternoon. I know you didn't understand—"

"I still don't understand," he swiftly cut in.

"I'm not a bad person, Chance."

"I don't think you are," he replied, his eyes quietly studying her troubled face.

Surprise lifted her eyebrows. "But you implied—"

Shaking his head, he said, "Lucy, you looked like the devil himself had taken a seat on your shoulder. What was I supposed to think? I was worried about you."

Worried about her? No. Lucy couldn't imagine Chance Delacroix being concerned about her. She was just a stranger passing through, a momentary disruption in his life. Still, like a child drawn to the magic of Christmas, Chance's words drew Lucinda to him.

"I know I overreacted. But—" Pausing, she spread her hands in a helpless gesture as she tried to assemble the best words to explain herself. "It wasn't Troy, personally, you see. He seemed like a very nice man."

"He is a very nice man. Even if he is my cousin."

She tried to swallow, then brought her hand to her throat when it refused to cooperate. "But all policemen aren't nice guys," she finally managed to say. "I know, because Richard was a policeman."

Rising to his feet, Chance closed the three steps that separated them. "Your ex-fiancé was a policeman?"

Her face solemn, Lucy nodded up at him. Once she'd left Chicago she'd planned to keep all this information to herself. But no matter what consequences came out of this, she couldn't let Chance go on thinking badly of her. She couldn't bear that.

"He was—is a homicide detective on the Chicago police force."

"I see," he said, his expression suddenly thoughtful.

"I doubt it. You're probably thinking that doesn't explain my reaction to Troy. But believe me, Chance, Richard turned out to be—well, he could be very unpleasant at times. He ruined my impression and my trust for the law. I know that doesn't exactly make sense, and the logical part of me knows that all law officials aren't like him, but I still can't seem to make the separation."

"Why didn't you tell me this before?"

Her mouth twisted wryly. "For the same reason you don't want to tell me things. It hurts."

Oh yes, Chance knew how the past, and retelling it, could hurt. As it had obviously hurt Lucinda, he thought grimly.

He didn't know what had prompted her to come to him and open up like this. But now that she had, Chance felt like a bastard. No, he more than felt like one. He *was* one. From the moment he'd picked Lucinda up from her wrecked car on the highway, he'd questioned her motives, her past, her future. He'd expected her to give out any information he wanted to know while, like a miser clutching his pennies, he'd held the biggest part of himself back from her. But then, he'd been doing that for more than ten years now. And the hell of it was, no one but Lucinda had pointed it out to him. Or maybe they had and she'd been the only one he'd listened to?

"So I guess I'll say good-night. I just wanted you to know how things were with me," Lucinda went on with a shrug of her shoulder. "I didn't want you thinking I had a suitcase full of stolen money stashed away in the car trunk and my being here would implicate you and your family."

Turning, she started toward the door. But before her hand reached the knob, Chance grabbed her shoulders and spun her back to him.

"I didn't really think that, Lucy," he said, his face bent close to hers. "I was just angry at you because you were being so damn closemouthed."

The warm light in his gray eyes made Lucinda believe him. It also made her quiver with longing. "Like you?" she couldn't help asking.

Chance couldn't be angry with her. How could he be, when everything inside of him wanted to pull her into his arms, cherish her warmth and her softness?

"It's been a long time since a woman has made me want to look twice," he admitted in a husky voice. "And now that you've come along, I don't know what to do about it."

At first Lucinda thought she'd heard him wrong, then when she realized she hadn't, her heart began to pound. "You—shouldn't do anything about it," she breathed.

His hands on her upper arms, he guided her back a step until she was pressed against the closed door. "Why? Because you're still in love with your policeman?"

The mere thought of loving Richard made her shiver with revulsion. "No! I'm not so sure I ever loved the man. At one time, I believed I did. But now I think I only accepted his engagement ring because I wanted security in my life. I've never had that before, you see."

"Maybe you wanted love to go along with that security," he suggested softly.

His hands were burning through her sweater, right down to the tips of her fingers. His lips, just inches away, were hypnotizing her, making it impossible to tear her eyes away from them. "I did want love. I'd wanted it very badly. But I didn't get it."

One hand lifted to touch her cheek, then tunneled into the side of her hair. "I didn't get it, either," he murmured.

His touch stirred Lucinda's senses, but it was his words that tugged at her heart. "But you—didn't you love Jolene? Didn't she love you back?"

All of a sudden, he moved away from her and went to stand by a single window. The drapes were parted, and beyond the glass panes, Christmas lights twinkled on the eave of the porch. Lucinda thought the cheerful decoration was an odd contrast to the twisted look of anguish on Chance's face.

"Oh, we were married," he conceded. "And we were in love, or so we thought. But I was barely twenty at the time and Jolene was nineteen. I think she was more in love with the idea of marriage and babies than she was with me."

"And you?"

"I wanted her. Physically. And back then I was too young to know physical desire wasn't what love was all about."

Lucinda didn't know what to say. All this time she'd believed he was harboring a great, deep-seated love for his dead wife. If that wasn't the case, why had he avoided women for so long? Why did he look so tormented now?

"Do you know how guilty that makes me feel?" he asked, when she failed to make a reply.

Frowning, Lucinda walked over to where he stood. "Why should you feel guilty? Jolene wanted to marry you, didn't she?"

A wan smile suddenly touched his features. "Oh yes. In fact, we eloped because she was afraid my parents would try to stop it." He looked at Lucinda. "You see, Jolene was from a poor family and she believed all the Delacroix resented her."

Lucinda couldn't imagine Dee being the sort of person to resent another just because they were less fortunate. But where their children were concerned, people often behaved differently. "Did your folks resent her?"

"No. But they didn't approve of us living in Amarillo."

A frown puckered her brow. "You didn't live here on the ranch?"

Chance shook his head. "Jolene didn't want to live around my family. Since she'd never had much of a home, she wanted one of her very own. So I tried my best to give her one. I got a job on a ranch just outside of the city and we rented a little house not far away from it. I worked during the days and went to college at night for a degree in agriculture."

"That must have been difficult," Lucinda said as she tried to picture a very young Chance struggling to become a husband and a man all at once.

He shrugged. "I'm sure you did the same thing. You obviously had to."

"Yes," she agreed. "But I only had the responsibility of taking care of myself."

With a long sigh, he turned his gaze back out toward the dark night. "Well, we made it somehow. Even up until it was time for the baby."

"The baby!" Lucinda gasped.

His face turned back to hers and Lucinda was suddenly haunted by the shadows she saw in his eyes.

"Yes. I figured Mother had already told you. Jolene died trying to have my child."

Stunned, Lucinda slowly shook her head. She'd expected him to say anything but that. "No. I didn't know. I—can't imagine such a thing happening to you."

His face full of bitterness, he said, "Neither could I. But there I was in the hospital waiting room, certain I was giving my wife the best of care, when the doctors came out and told me she was gone and so was the baby. A girl. Perfectly formed, but gone. Like her mother."

Lucinda's heart squeezed with pain for him. In less than two years, he'd lost his wife and child, then his father. How had he endured such pain?

"What happened to her and the baby?" she asked.

One of his shoulders lifted, then fell. "Oh, the doctors gave me all sorts of medical excuses, most of which I couldn't understand. I just knew that something had caused her to hemorrhage so violently they couldn't stop it. At the time, I didn't care to hear their reasons or explanations, anyway. Jolene and the baby were dead. As far as I was concerned I'd killed them."

"Chance!" she gasped. "That's crazy."

"Maybe so. But I'm the one who made Jolene pregnant in the first place."

"And that's supposed to make you a murderer?"

Pinching the bridge of his nose, he sighed, then said, "I've always thought so."

Determined to reach him, Lucinda grabbed both his hands and held them tightly. "Then it's high time you stopped," she told him. "You need to put all of that behind you—leave it in the past where it belongs."

His eyes lifted and locked with hers as slowly his fingers folded around hers and squeezed. "Do you think you're the woman who can make me put it all in the past?"

She wasn't expecting him to ask such a thing. Even so, the moment her heart had heard the question it had known the answer. She wanted to be that woman. His woman. The woman to give him true love and happiness. But that wasn't possible. Not with Richard hanging like a dangerous cloud just behind her shoulder.

"Chance, I'm not—I can't be that sort of woman to you—or any man."

"Why not?"

With an anguished groan, she turned away from him. "Because it isn't possible. Because I can't forget—"

Before she could get it out of her mouth, he snatched her arm and spun her back around to him.

"You just told me I needed to forget the past. Put it behind me. Why can't you? Or is this a case of do as I say, not as I do?"

"This is different," she said, her voice full of torment. "I have reasons to steer clear of a relationship with a man."

His hands came up to gently frame her face. "For years I've had lots of reasons hanging in front of my eyes. Now you've come along and made them all look not so important anymore."

Oh, dear God, he shouldn't be saying this to her, she thought. And she shouldn't be wanting to hear it. But her heart reveled in his sweet confession, glowed with a love as warm and bright as the Christmas candle burning on the living room mantel.

"I'm glad, Chance." With one hand she reached up and traced his cheek with the tips of her fingers. "You deserve to be happy. But not with me."

"You might be wrong about that, Lucy," he murmured. "In fact, I'm pretty sure you're wrong."

As if she were under some sort of spell, she stood totally still and watched his face bend to hers. "Chance—"

"Don't talk, Lucy. Just close your eyes and let me kiss you. The way I've wanted to kiss you since the first night I saw you."

The last was said against her lips, and by then Lucinda had already surrendered to him. Like butter sliding down a stack of warm pancakes, she melted against him, opened her mouth to him and welcomed the sweet invasion of his tongue.

The smell of him, the feel of him had already become achingly familiar to her, and knowing these moments would have to last her a lifetime, she held on to him tightly. Urgently.

By the time Chance finally lifted his lips, the room was spinning around Lucinda's head. Her breaths were coming in short pants and her knees were close to buckling beneath her.

"You say you don't want a relationship with me," Chance murmured, his lips pressing tiny kisses down the side of her throat. "But your body is telling me something else."

It was telling Lucinda something, too. She wanted to make love to this man. That was bad enough. But even worse, she realized she not only wanted to give him her body, she wanted to give him her heart. Something she'd vowed to guard with her very life.

"Chance, you don't know—"

Her words were smothered as his mouth found hers once again. At the same time, his hands delved beneath the hem of her sweater, spread upward against her back, then slowly inched forward to her breasts.

Once his fingers closed around their fullness, Lucinda was lost. Arching her hips against his, she urged him to deepen the kiss. Even though his teeth were grazing hers, his tongue was already exploring every intimate curve of her mouth.

Never had anything felt this good, or this right to her. And maybe that was the thing that frightened Lucinda the most. She was rapidly losing herself to Chance. She was letting another man take control of her again and she knew she must never let that happen.

Twisting away and turning her back to him, she gulped in deep, ragged breaths. "I'm not going to let you change my mind," she whispered hoarsely.

Long moments passed without a word from him. Finally, unable to keep her eyes off him, she turned to see him smiling at her. It was a knowing smile, full of pleasure and a dash of smugness.

"I think I already have, Lucy."

Terrified that he might try to prove it, Lucinda stepped around him and rushed out the door. She wasn't going to give him another opportunity to work his charms on her, she vowed as she ran down the hallway to her bedroom. Because next time, she might not be strong enough to resist.

Chapter Nine

The next afternoon Lucinda held a pattern piece up to Sarah Jane and carefully eyed the fit.

"This will drape over to your left shoulder and tie in a knot like this," Lucinda said to Sarah Jane.

"And that will make a collar?" the younger woman asked.

Nodding, Lucinda placed the thin piece of paper on the dining table, picked up another one and fitted it against Sarah Jane's midriff. "The rest of the bodice will fit tightly. I think the whole thing will look young and romantic and flirty. What do you think?"

The younger woman sighed with pleasure. "Oh, Lucy, you're a genius. You seem to have known exactly the sort of clothes I was looking for without me even telling you!"

"That's why she does that for a living, Sarah Jane," Dee spoke up from across the kitchen. "She's good at it."

"So what sort of fabric will this dress be made of?" Sarah Jane asked as Lucinda carefully continued to fit all the pattern pieces against her.

"Something that will give the skirt a pretty flow. Maybe silk georgette. A peach-colored print, I think. A solid color might make it look too severe. Unless you'd like something else?"

"No. Oh, no! Whatever you say, I trust you completely," Sarah Jane assured her.

"Lucy, you've worked all morning and nearly half of the afternoon on those patterns," Dee said. "Put them away and take a break. There's no need for you to get them all done so quickly."

"That's right," Sarah Jane said. "Like we told you, what you don't finish you can mail back to us. Or better yet, you can stay with us longer. Like until my wedding in May."

Lucinda laughed at the younger woman's outrageous suggestion. "As much as I'd love to see your wedding, Sarah Jane, I've got to be heading on. It's about time I found a place of my own and started back to work."

"Well, I don't know why you can't just make your home around here, close to us," Sarah Jane insisted.

"I'd like that, too, Sarah Jane," Dee said as she poured flour into a big mixing bowl. "But how could Lucinda make a living around here?"

Sarah Jane hopped up onto a stool at the breakfast counter. "Easy," she said. "Every few months she could take her things to Dallas. They have those big fashion buying shows over there all the time. And from what I've heard, everyone from department store buyers to small boutiques purchase merchandise at them."

"Hmm. That's not a bad idea," Dee said thoughtfully as she dumped more ingredients into the bowl. "What do you think, Lucy? Think you'd like being a Texan?"

Lucy began gathering her patterns, scissors and silk straight pins and putting them away in her workbasket. Sarah Jane's idea had caught Lucinda by surprise. Firstly, because it was such a good one, and secondly it was something she wished she could really do. It would be wonderful to live somewhere nearby, to have these two women for friends. She'd never been around anyone she felt more at home with. And she knew she was going to miss them terribly once she left here. But that was the way it had to be.

"I've never really thought about living in Texas," she told Dee. "But I believe I'll do better with my work on the West Coast."

"I wish you didn't feel that way," Sarah Jane said to Lucinda. "I think you'd like it here."

Lucinda *knew* she would like it here. But until she was certain that Richard wouldn't harm her or her friends, she couldn't really begin to make a home for herself. And right now she wasn't sure of anything. He might be on the road looking for her, and if she led him here to this ranch, she would never forgive herself.

A few minutes later, after the women had shared a cup of coffee, they all got busy making Christmas cookies. Lucinda had never had a reason to do any baking for Christmas before and she was surprised at how much enjoyment she was getting from cutting the dough into stars, wreaths, and Christmas trees, then decorating them with sprinkles and frostings.

She was standing at the kitchen counter, flour on her face and in her hair when Chance came in the back door. The weather had turned cold and cloudy again and he'd been working in it for most of the day. Before he'd stepped into the kitchen he'd been wondering if he would ever feel warm again. But now the sight of Lucinda in a pair of tight blue jeans and a pink shirt with the sleeves rolled up to her elbows was quickly filling him with heat.

He hadn't seen her at breakfast. Then right before lunch, he'd gotten a trailer loaded with hay stuck in one of the back pastures. By the time Chance and one of the other hands had pulled it out, he'd skipped eating altogether. He'd also missed seeing Lucinda. And after what had transpired between them last night, that wasn't something Chance had planned to do.

"What's cooking?" he asked to no one in general as he pulled off his hat and wiped his muddy boots on a rug by the door.

"Christmas cookies," Sarah Jane told him.

"Already?" he asked.

Lucinda could feel him coming up behind her, but she kept her attention firmly on what she was doing. She didn't want to send any sort of signal his way. She wanted to give him the impression that last night and the moments they'd shared in each other's arms were something she didn't intend to repeat.

"It's only two more days until Christmas Eve," Dee pointed out to him. "We've got to get on with it, to finish all the baking I plan to do."

Reaching over Lucinda's shoulder, Chance dipped his finger into the stiff cookie dough. Lucinda twisted her head around to see him eating the raw dough from his fingers. It was the first time she'd seen him since last night. Memories of his kisses, the feel of his rough-skinned hands moving so tenderly against her flooded her thoughts and darkened her eyes with unbidden desire.

"Mmm. That's pretty good stuff."

She jerked her gaze back on the work in front of her. "It will be when it's baked," she told him while trying to keep her voice as casual as she could manage.

"And you're not to get into these, or the others," Sarah Jane spoke up as she pulled a tray of freshly baked cookies from the oven. "These are going to the church tonight for refreshments."

Chance frowned at his sister. "Tonight isn't church night."

"Charles Delacroix!" Dee scolded. "Have you forgotten about the Christmas pageant? Sarah Jane and I will be singing a duet. I know I told you this morning."

She probably had, Chance thought wryly. But he'd had other things on his mind. Like what he was going to do about Lucinda and the way he was beginning to feel about her. He wanted her. And she wanted him, or so her kisses had told him. But did that mean he was really ready to put all the past behind him? He'd married one woman and lost her. And since then he'd vowed he would never set himself up for that kind of hellish pain again. But Lucinda was doing something to him. She was blurring his memories, making him believe the future could be different.

"I guess I didn't hear you," he told his mother, then winking at Lucinda, he reached over her shoulder once again and broke the point off a star she was sprinkling with red sugar.

"Chance! You've ruined that one!" she exclaimed.

He popped the point into his mouth and chewed with obvious pleasure. "It isn't ruined," he assured her with a chuckle. "Four-pointed stars taste just as good as five-pointed ones."

Sarah Jane groaned as she arranged some of the already cooled cookies into a round tin. "Keep your paws to yourself, Chance. We don't come down to the barn and interfere with your work."

He crossed the room to the coffee machine and poured a mugful. "I wish somebody had come to help. I was stuck half the morning, then when I finally got the tractor back to the ranch, a water line had frozen beneath the horse barn. We've spent all afternoon digging it up."

Dee handed him a freshly made ham sandwich. "Well, I don't know which is worse. Winter, when everything is frozen. Or summer, when everything is dry and roasted."

Chance swallowed a sip of the hot coffee and found himself wishing his mother and sister were out of the room. More than anything he'd like to go over to Lucinda and kiss the dab of flour from her cheek, nuzzle her neck and draw her back against him until every curve of her body was touching his.

"You are coming to the pageant tonight, aren't you? Your sister and I are counting on you being there."

Realizing his mother was talking to him, Chance turned his head in her direction. "Of course, I'll go. I wouldn't miss seeing you and Sarah Jane dressed up as angels."

Dee smiled happily at him. "Good. Then you can bring Lucinda with you. Since Sarah Jane and I have to be there very early, there's no need for her to ride with us and have to sit for more than an hour before the program starts."

Hearing her name mentioned in their plans, Lucinda twisted around to look at the two of them. "I didn't realize I was going anywhere."

Chance smiled at her. "Sure you are. You're coming with me. And make sure you're ready by six."

He put down the coffee mug and carried the rest of his sandwich out the back door.

Once he was out of sight, Lucinda released a long sigh. How in the world was she going to handle this?

A little after six that evening, Lucinda sat staring out the pickup window, her fingers absently toying with the pearl choker she wore around her neck. It had been a long time since she'd been to church, and she'd missed it greatly. But after Richard had begun threatening her and following her every move, Lucinda had stopped going anywhere that wasn't absolutely necessary.

For the past months, she'd only left her apartment to go to work or the grocery market. And just doing that had made her a nervous wreck. It made her furious to think how her life had gradually been taken away from her, narrowed down to just the basic necessities. She'd nearly forgotten what it was like to dress up and go out to celebrate Christmas or any special occasion.

"If you'd quit frowning, you'd look perfect," Chance told her as he turned the pickup onto the main highway toward Friona.

She glanced over at him and told herself not to be impressed. But she was anyway. He was wearing western-cut khaki trousers, a white shirt, and a brown leather jacket. None of which were special, or dressy. In fact, the jacket looked as if he'd had it for a long time. The leather was scarred and worn in several places. But it matched his old black hat, and with his dark, good looks and lean, rugged body, he made it all look special.

"I'll do my best to look happier," she told him.

"You didn't want to come with me tonight. I can tell."

Lucinda smoothed her hand nervously down the lap of her deep green skirt. "I haven't said anything of the sort."

"No. You haven't said *anything*. That tells me a lot."

Frowning, she turned her gaze back to the windshield in front of her. "It should simply be telling you I'm all talked out."

"It's funny how you should say that. For a long time now I've hated talking. Mother and Sarah were constantly chattering and they always expected me to join in. I would, but it was an effort at times. The ranch hands were always swapping stories and gossip and they would include me in their conversations. I gritted my teeth and said as little as I could get by with. Now you've come along and picked and prodded at me until you've got all sorts of words comin' out of my mouth."

She looked at him again, this time her lips parted with surprise. "I haven't picked and prodded at you."

"Then what have you done to me?"

A warm flush seeped into her cheeks. "Nothing. And I don't intend to. I told you that last night."

Chance's gaze traveled over the beautiful picture she made in her white silk blouse and Christmas green skirt. "If we weren't on our way to church, I'd pull this truck over and prove you wrong."

Just the mention of being back in his arms shook Lucinda all the way down to her toes. "Well, we are on our way to church," she reminded him primly, then shot him an annoyed glance. "You really want to know what I've done to you?"

"I'm all ears," he said, enjoying this time alone with her.

"I've simply wakened your libido. And now you're beginning to think I'm someone special."

She sounded weary, even a little cynical. Chance wanted to shake her. "Oh, my libido was always awake. I just never wanted to acknowledge it. Till I found you."

Lucinda started to point out that he hadn't found her. But she stopped herself. He had found her. Rescued her. And now he thought they were headed toward something more intimate between them. How had this happened? she wondered miserably.

"I've been thinking a lot about last night," he went on, "and some of the things you said to me."

Her head bent, she fixed her gaze on the toes of her black dress boots. "I said them because I—meant them." Sud-

denly she turned on the seat and allowed her eyes to glide
over the shadowed angles of his face. It seemed incredible
that this man had come to mean so much to her. She'd only
known him for a few days. Yet she felt closer to him than
she'd ever felt to anyone in her life. "And I do truly hope
you can put Jolene and everything that happened back then,
behind you. If you do, I know you can be happy again."

Chance *was* becoming happy again and she was the reason. That much he already knew. What he didn't know was
how to make Lucinda believe that she could be happy with
him.

So far she seemed determined to follow the course she'd
mapped out for herself when she'd first left Chicago. But
there were still a couple of days left until Christmas, he told
himself, and from now until then he planned to use that time
to do some mighty big persuading.

The church the Delacroix attended was some eight miles
away from the ranch house. By the time Chance and Lucinda arrived, the parking lot around the brown brick
building was almost full.

Inside, the wooden pews were quickly filling with people
of all ages. The two of them found a seat next to James,
Sarah Jane's fiancé. He was a quiet young man with light
brown hair and a slender build. Lucinda had never met him
before, but from the few minutes of conversation they
shared with him before the start of the program, she decided Sarah Jane was going to be in good hands.

The Christmas play turned out to be a much bigger pro-
duction than Lucinda had imagined it would be. Several
times throughout the program, she couldn't help but re-
mark to Chance on the beautiful settings, which had been
made to look like the streets and buildings of Old Bethle-
hem.

Chance enjoyed watching the story of the birth of Christ being acted out in word and song on the small stage. Though he'd seen it many times down through the years, he always looked forward to seeing it again. Yet this time, with Lucinda sitting next to him, her face shining with awe and reverence, it had all taken on a special meaning to him.

When Dee and Sarah Jane stepped onto the stage to sing "Silent Night" Lucinda couldn't stop herself from reaching over and curling her small hand around Chance's.

"You must be so proud of them," she whispered, her eyes suddenly misting over with emotion.

Tightening his fingers around hers, he smiled. "Very proud, Lucy."

He wanted to tell her that he was proud of her, too. Proud that she was sitting here beside him, sharing this special time with him and his family. But the feeling was so new to him, so fresh and tender that he didn't know how to put it into words. Instead, he held on to her hand, while inside him, the last haunting memories of the past faded away.

A few minutes later, the program ended and the socializing began. Chance took Lucinda over to the refreshment table, where they were immediately swamped by his friends and relatives. One being his cousin, Troy.

This time when Lucinda saw him, she knew there was nothing to fear and she smiled warmly as he shook her hand.

"It's nice to see you again, Miss Lambert. Have you tried your car since Mike returned it to you?"

Lucinda glanced at Chance, who seemed to be watching her closely. "No. But Chance did. Other than having a tire blown out, he says it didn't seem to be hurt."

"You're lucky," Troy told her. "That was a nasty ditch you drove into. You and the car could have ended up in a bad way."

"Yes, I was lucky," she agreed. Over the rim of her punch glass, she glanced at Chance. "Especially lucky that Chance rescued me."

Troy gave his cousin a pointed grin. "Looks to me like Chance is the lucky one," he told Lucinda. "The only thing he ever gets to rescue is a sick calf or cow. Beautiful women aren't his forte."

Smiling down at Lucinda, Chance asked, "Did I tell you that besides being the sheriff of Parmer County my cousin is also its biggest flirt?"

Tonight, for the first time in ages, she felt like a woman again. She felt wanted and desired and the nearest thing to happiness that she could imagine. Chance actually seemed proud to bring her into his circle of family and friends and she couldn't help loving him for that.

"No," she answered Chance's question. "I don't believe you told me that about him."

Laughing, Troy slapped Chance on the shoulder. "What did you tell her about me, buddy?"

Chance put his arm around Lucinda's shoulders and edged her away from the young sheriff. "Not anything that would ruin your reputation, cuz."

They moved on through the crowd, where Chance introduced her to several neighbors, an uncle, another cousin and a second cousin. Stories and news were swapped, a table of food eaten, and Merry Christmas wished to everyone before the crowd finally broke up and headed home.

On their way back to the ranch, Lucinda leaned her head against the seat and sighed with contentment.

Chance glanced away from the highway to look at her. "Did you have a good time?"

A wide smile curved her lips. "Oh, yes. The play was so beautiful and your mother and sister's duet was wonderful. And all your friends and relatives were so—"

"Hayseed?" he asked with a chuckle.

She grimaced. "There's nothing wrong with being hayseed or homespun. I liked all of them. They made me feel so welcome and a part of everything."

"I'm glad."

The quietness and the fact that they were alone again began to settle in on Lucinda. Trying her best to ignore it, she looked at him and smiled again. "Thank you for bringing me. I'll never forget this night."

Chance would always remember it, too. He would only have to think of Christmas and Lucinda would be there in his mind. After this week, he doubted he would ever be able to separate the two. And what would it be like without Lucinda this time next year? he wondered. Where would she be? What would she be doing? Spending her Christmas with some other man and his family?

It was a good thing they were already in the driveway at the front of the house; otherwise, Chance would have simply stopped the pickup on the side of the highway.

"Chance, what are you doing?" she gasped as he grabbed both her hands and tugged her toward him.

"Making damn sure you don't forget tonight, or me," he growled softly.

Forget him? How could she, when her heart, every fiber of her being seemed to be beating just for him?

One hand slid into her hair, cupped the back of her head and urged her face up to his. Lucinda couldn't deny him. A soft sigh parted her lips and caressed his face with a silent invitation.

Groaning, Chance bent his head and closed the small gap between their lips. Lucinda lifted her arms around his neck, smoothed her hands across his back and sank herself into the heat of his kiss.

Chance had never tasted anything as sweet and intoxicating as Lucinda. Each time he touched her, kissed her, it was like a whole new journey for him. She hadn't just awakened his sex drive. No, she'd shaken up everything inside him. And where Chance had only been existing before, now he felt alive and thirsty for all the things he'd been without. The touch and the love of a woman. Hope for tomorrow and the next, and the next.

Breaking the contact between their lips, he gasped, "Oh, Lucy, Lucy! I want to make love to you."

More than anything, Lucinda wanted to simply draw his lips back down on hers, guide his hands to her breasts and let her body show him how much she wanted the same thing. But she couldn't do that. She had a dark, unsettled past. She had to move on from here, make sure it never followed her or spilled over onto Chance or his family.

"Chance, I—don't go around having sex with—"

Suddenly his hands were cupping her cheeks, his gray eyes were delving into hers. "Lucinda, you're not hearing me. I didn't say I wanted to have sex with you. I said I wanted to make love to you."

Was he trying to say that he loved her? Both joy and fear burst inside her, making an anguished groan slip from her throat.

Laying her palms against both sides of his face, she said softly, "I'm not the person you think I am, Chance. You—"

Suddenly his hands were on her shoulders, urging her down on the pickup seat. "I don't want to hear about your past, Lucy. I want to know if you want to make love to me, too?"

With the heat of his body covering hers, his finger delicately outlining the edge of her lips, she couldn't lie to him. How could she say no, when all she could think about was the fire in her body and the exquisite pleasure of having Chance cool the flames?

"Yes. I do want to make love to you," she whispered truthfully.

A groan, exultant and deep, ripped from his throat and then his mouth was back on hers, tasting, teasing, begging her to show him exactly what she wanted.

She returned his kiss with a fierce passion. At the same time, Chance reached for the buttons on her blouse. Before he could get the last one undone, he lowered his head to the curves mounded above the cups of her lacy bra.

Lucinda gasped as his teeth grazed her soft skin, nipped delicately at her nipples through the thin French lace. Fire was racing along her veins, mounting an attack on her senses and creating an ache inside her such as she'd never known.

"Oh, Lucy. My sweet love," he mouthed against her, his fingers fumbling with the button on her waistband.

Far beyond resisting him now, Lucinda reached to help him. At the same moment, the sweep of headlights flashed the cab of the pickup.

Dazed, they looked at each other as though neither of them were sure of where they were. Finally it was Chance who cursed under his breath.

"It's Mother and Sarah Jane."

Galvanized by his words, Lucinda snatched her blouse together and tumbled out of the pickup. Ignoring the pain in her ankle, she raced into the house and down the hallway to her room long before the other two women parked the car.

Chance, however, remained in the truck. Like a man who'd been running for miles, his forehead dropped against the steering wheel and his lungs sucked in long breaths of cold night air.

By the time he felt collected enough to go in, the lights in the house had long gone out and his hands had grown cold. But there was warmth in his heart. And for a man who'd been close to death for nearly ten years, that was a hell of a feeling.

Chapter Ten

"I am dead on my feet," Sarah Jane groaned.

"I think Dr. Campbell would tell me I've overdone it," Lucinda replied, flopping down onto one end of the couch and flexing her aching ankle.

The two women had spent the entire morning and a big part of the afternoon making a shopping trip to Amarillo and back. They'd purchased several yards of material for Sarah Jane's new clothes and at the last minute, Lucinda had decided to purchase a Christmas gift for Chance.

After what had happened between the two of them last night in the pickup, Lucinda wasn't sure if giving him a gift would be the right thing to do. She didn't want him to get the wrong idea and think he was becoming special to her.

He has become special to you, Lucinda. The inner voice taunted her and dared her to deny it. But Lucinda couldn't argue with the little voice, or herself. Chance had somehow managed to fill her heart. Somewhere between the moment he'd carried her out of her wrecked car and now, she'd fallen in love with him.

She knew it was foolish and crazy and something she could never hope to act upon, but it was there in her heart anyway. As for the gift, she couldn't let Christmas pass without giving him something.

A knock at the front door caught both women's attention.

"I wonder who that could be in the middle of the afternoon?" Sarah Jane mumbled as she pushed herself off the couch and headed to the door.

Seconds later, Sarah Jane turned away from the door with a huge Christmas bouquet and a bubbling smile on her face. "It was the florist truck! Look at this!"

"James really splurged on you," Lucinda exclaimed.

"Sarah Jane, who was at the door?" Dee asked as she stepped into the room. The moment she saw the bouquet, she gasped with surprise. "Wow! Someone felt mighty generous! If James sent you those, Chance is going to kick his butt. You know he thinks you two kids should be saving your money."

Sarah Jane set the arrangement on the coffee table in front of the couch. "Chance is going to keep his feet and his opinions to himself," she said, quickly prowling through the holly and red carnations for a card.

Dee laughed and winked at Lucinda.

"This little white bear is adorable," Lucinda said, touching the button nose of the stuffed animal nestled among the leaves and flowers.

Sarah Jane finally found the card, then immediately gasped with surprise as she read it. "This isn't for me! They're for you, Lucy!"

Stunned, Lucinda's head began to wag back and forth. "Me? But they can't be. No one around here would send me something like this? No one even knows me!"

Giggling at the mistaken assumption that James had sent them to her, Sarah Jane handed the card to her. "Well, someone did."

"Merry Christmas, Lucinda," she read aloud. "Is that all? Does the envelope have the sender's name on it?"

Sarah Jane shook her head as she flopped the square of white paper over in her hand. "Not a thing."

"Well, perhaps it was Chance," Dee spoke up. "Maybe he wanted to do something nice for Lucy."

"Oh, no! These aren't from Chance," Lucinda quickly countered. "I don't think your son is the bouquet type."

"Lucy's right. I've never known of Chance sending flowers to anyone. Besides you, Mother."

Dee shook her head. "It beats me. Unless the—"

"The flowers are from someone Lucinda met at church last night," Sarah Jane finished her mother's sentence. "Troy probably. He always was a romantic."

Lucinda didn't think Troy was the sender. She'd gotten the impression that the sheriff considered her Chance's property, and she'd said or done nothing to make him think otherwise. No. The flowers were from someone else. And the sick fear in the pit of her stomach told her that some-one else was probably Richard.

"Troy or not," Dee said wistfully, "it's a beautiful Christmas gift. Too bad Doc didn't think of sending me one."

"I'll put in a hint for you, Mother. The flowers will go perfectly with that diamond engagement ring he's getting for you."

Dee waved her hand airily. "That old man isn't getting me a ring! I wouldn't take it anyway."

Sarah Jane laughed, but Lucinda didn't. Her mind was in turmoil as she stared at the flowers and the little white bear.

"Oh, yes, you will, Mother," Sarah Jane went on. "You'd die before you let Doc give that ring to some other woman."

Dee stuck her chin out. "He doesn't want any other woman. He wants me."

Laughing, Sarah Jane gave her mother an affectionate hug. Across from them, Lucinda rose to her feet.

"If you two will excuse me for a while I think I'll go for a walk," she said.

Her expression suddenly serious, Sarah Jane quickly pointed out, "You've been on your ankle too much already, Lucy. Don't you think you need to rest?"

Lucinda couldn't rest. Nor would she be able to, until she was absolutely sure Richard hadn't sent her those flowers.

Pulling on her coat, she said, "I'm fine. I'd just like some fresh air. I think I'll go look in on Caesar and make sure he's doing all right."

Since the weather had turned out to be another cold and cloudy day, there hadn't been much thawing. Snowdrifts were still piled next to most of the buildings and the fence posts.

With her head bent and her arms wrapped around her waist, Lucinda picked her way around the slushy puddles of ice and water. The cold air helped clear the fatigue of driving back from Amarillo, but it did little to push away the nagging fear that Richard had somehow tracked her here to the ranch.

"Have you lost something? Or are you just counting all the piles of cow manure you've stepped in?"

Lucinda looked up to see Chance approaching her on Traveler, the horse she'd ridden with him. Had that been only three days ago? No, surely it had been longer. So much had happened since then. Chance and his family had changed her. Her heart, her wants and dreams were so very different now.

"I'm trying to stay out of the mud holes," she told him.

He reined the horse to a stop and stepped down from the saddle. Lucinda stood to one side of the path and waited until he was standing next to her. Even though her mind carried a constant vision of him, it never compared to the real thing. The shape of his long, muscular legs were evident beneath the blue jeans he'd jammed into the tops of his black cowboy boots. The brown suede sheep-lined coat he was wearing made his broad shoulders appear that much wider. Although he'd been clean shaven for their outing at church last night, he'd obviously neglected the chore today. Black whiskers shadowed his jaws and chin and upper lip, giving him a hell-for-leather look. It suited him. Just as the ruggedness of these great Texas plains suited him, she thought.

"I see you and Sarah Jane made it safely back from Amarillo. Did you have a good time?"

It was such a simple question, but his asking it meant more than she could possibly ever tell him. To think that he wanted her to be happy, that he wanted her day to be a good one, filled her with an undescribable joy.

"Yes, I did. Sarah Jane is such fun to be with. I'm going to miss her terribly once I leave here."

So she was still planning on leaving after Christmas, Chance thought. Why did that surprise him? She'd been saying that very thing all along. Because, damn it, he argued with himself, she'd very nearly made love to him last night. If his mother and sister hadn't shown up when they did, nothing would have stopped them. Just thinking about it now left a ball of heat in the pit of his stomach.

"Are you going somewhere in particular?" he asked.

"I was going to visit Caesar. Where are you going?"

"I was coming to fetch you."

She glanced up at his face, which was partially shadowed by the brim of his hat. Nothing on his features hinted that he was expecting her to mention flowers.

"Me?"

Taking her by the arm, Chance began to walk her toward another barn situated several yards beyond the one that housed the horses.

"Yeah, there's something I want you to see."

Inside the building two other cowboys were spreading alfalfa in a long hay manger. They glanced around as Chance and Lucinda walked nearby.

"We're gonna check on the new additions, guys," Chance told them.

"They're doin' fine, Chance. Already been eatin' like they were starved to death," one of the men called to him.

Chance gave him a thumbs-up signal, then guided Lucinda to a pen toward the back of the building.

At first, all Lucinda could see was a big black cow chewing a mouthful of hay.

"Look behind her on the ground."

Lucinda bent her head in order to see under the cow's feet, then squealed with soft delight as she spotted the two baby calves.

"There's two of them! And they look exactly alike! Isn't it unusual for a cow to have twins?"

Resting his forearms across the top board of the pen, Chance smiled at her excitement over the newborn calves. "It happens about as often as it does to humans."

"Then it's a special event," she said, her eyes still on the matching pair of calves. "When were they born?"

"About forty minutes ago. I've been down here watching her the biggest part of the day. We thought we were going to have to pull the first one, but once she had him, the little heifer wasn't any problem at all.''

Lucinda was amazed. Looking up at Chance she asked, ''You mean this cow gave birth less than an hour ago and she's already up eating?''

Chance nodded. ''If everything goes all right during birth, a cow gets up immediately afterward and begins to clean her baby. Before the calf hardly has time to dry, it will stand and begin to nurse.''

Marveling at the whole idea, Lucinda glanced back at the babies. ''A few days ago, I didn't know what living on a ranch meant, or what it was like to be around animals.'' Feeling suddenly foolish, she shook her head, then looked up at Chance. ''Of course you know that. I guess what I'm trying to say is thank you for wanting to show it all to me.''

Reaching over, Chance slid his hand down her arm, then curled his fingers around hers. ''I've never met a woman like you, Lucy. Such simple things please you.''

Disturbed by the sudden intimacy of his touch, Lucinda's eyes dropped from his. ''That's because I'm a simple person, Chance.''

He shook his head. ''No. You're not simple at all. You're special.''

''I don't want you to think that.''

''Why not?''

She didn't answer immediately. Chance tightened his hold on her hand and drew her a step closer to him. ''Why not, Lucy?'' he repeated.

Lifting her eyes to him, she said, ''Because it would be better if you'd just think of me as your friend.''

''I do think of you as my friend. My closest friend. And a whole lot more,'' he murmured.

Lucinda's heart began to thud heavily beneath her breast. "Did you—" She broke off, swallowed, then started again. "Someone sent me flowers. Was it you?"

As soon as the question was out, Lucinda knew there wasn't any need for him to answer. The look of total surprise on his face assured Lucinda that he hadn't been the anonymous sender.

"Someone sent you flowers, but you don't know who?"

Her spirit plummeting to her feet, Lucinda shook her head. "The card wasn't signed."

He grimaced. "Well, it wasn't me," he said, then his eyes gently probed her face. "Do you wish it had been?"

Of course she did! That's what made the whole thing even worse!

"Don't ask me that, Chance," she said with an anguished groan.

The tug of his hands urged her closer, until their bodies touched, their breaths mingled. "For whatever it's worth, Lucy, I wish I had sent you those flowers. But right now a whole garden of them couldn't begin to tell you what you're doing to me."

"Chance, we're ready to go doctor that bull," a cowboy called from the other side of the barn. "You wanta take the Jeep?"

Cursing under his breath, he glanced over Lucinda's shoulder at his hired hand. "Yeah, I'll be there in a minute or two, Tim."

Looking back down at Lucinda, he said, "There's fourthousand acres on this ranch, but for some reason we always seem to have an audience."

Which was probably for the best, Lucinda thought. Otherwise, she might be tempted to give in to him. "It— doesn't matter. I need to get back to the house and help your mother with supper anyway."

With a sigh of frustration, Chance caught her hand and began to lead her back outside to where Traveler stood tied at a fence post.

As he loosened the girth on the saddle, Lucinda's hand closed around the gift she'd slipped into her coat pocket before she'd left the house. She had brought it with her, thinking if she ran into him down here at the barn she would give it to him now, instead of waiting until Christmas Day, when the house would be full of family and friends. That day would be her last day here on the D Bar D. She didn't think she would be in a gift-giving mood then.

"Chance?"

Glancing away from the breast harness he was unbuckling, he was stunned to see Lucinda extending a brightly wrapped package toward him. "What's this?"

She placed it in his hands. "My Christmas present to you."

"I didn't expect one."

Lucinda hadn't expected a lot of the things she'd gotten from him, either. Maybe when she was far away in California this gift would let him know that she really did care about him, that even though she was gone, he was the most special thing that had ever come into her life.

Smiling gently up at him, she said, "I know you didn't expect it. But I thought you deserved something for rescuing me."

A grin suddenly spread across his face and he tore into the paper like a kid who knew he was about to get what he'd always wanted.

"Spurs!" he exclaimed, his voice conveying just how much she'd surprised him.

She took the torn paper and box from him. "I thought all cowboys liked spurs. And the man at the tack store assured me these were a good sturdy pair. I started to get a pair with fancy silver on them, but then I figured you would only put them up and never use them. And I want you to wear these."

He ran his fingers over the basket-weave design on the leather strap, then twirled each of the small brass rowels.

"You do wear spurs, don't you, Chance?" she asked when he failed to say anything.

Laughing, he grabbed her and hugged her to him. "I have about twenty pairs of spurs, Lucy. But not one pair are as special as these!"

A lump suddenly collected in her throat. "You're not just saying that to be nice?"

Laughing again, he set her from him and quickly began to fasten the spurs around his boot heels. "I'm not a particularly nice man, Lucy. I thought you knew that by now."

Moving back a few steps, he grinned and asked, "How do I look?"

He looked incredibly like the man she loved. But she couldn't tell him that. Not now. Not ever. With a sad little ache in her heart, she smiled at him. "You look like a man with a new pair of spurs."

A few yards away from them, the hired hands pulled up in the Jeep. Ignoring their honk, Chance bent his head and kissed her on the cheek. "Thank you, Lucy."

"You're welcome, Chance."

Stepping away from her, he gathered up Traveler's reins and started toward the barn and the waiting men. Halfway there, he looked over his shoulder and waved to her. "Wait till the guys see these," he shouted to her. "They're gonna be as jealous as hell."

She smiled and waved back at him. Yet the moment she turned and started toward the house, hot tears oozed from her eyes and rolled down her cheeks.

Giving Chance the spurs had been her way of saying goodbye to him. And nothing had ever hurt her so much.

Lucinda was setting the table for supper when the telephone rang. Dee, who was busy at the cookstove, asked Lucinda to answer it.

"If it's for me," she said, "I'll have to call them back. And if they want Sarah Jane, she's gone to see James."

Lucinda hurried over to the ringing phone. "I'll take care of it," she told Dee, then to the receiver she said, "Hello. Delacroix's residence."

"Well, isn't that something. Just out of nowhere I call a ranch in West Texas and I hear your voice. I'd say that had to be pure fate, honey."

Her first instinct was to slam the phone down, but she knew she couldn't. He would only ring the number again. Lucinda gripped the phone as the room began to whirl around her head. These past few days, she'd prayed night and day that she would never hear Richard's voice again. Apparently God hadn't heard her.

"You sent the flowers, didn't you?" she asked in a hoarse whisper.

A malicious laugh came back in her ear. "Why sure I did, baby. You know I couldn't let Christmas go by without giving you something. And I plan to give you more than just flowers. A whole lot more."

Desperately Lucinda darted a glance at Dee and was thankful to see she was busy digging for something in the refrigerator and wasn't listening.

"How did you find me?" she murmured under her breath.

"It wasn't hard at all, once I put the fear of God into that friend of yours."

"Molly? What did you do to her?" she demanded, uncaring now if Dee heard her or not.

"She's fine," Richard snorted. "But those kids of hers weren't gonna be if she hadn't spilled her guts and told me where you were!"

My God, he'd threatened to harm Molly's children, she thought sickly. The man was totally deranged!

"What do you want, Richard?" she whispered fiercely.

He made a tsking noise. "Lucinda, living among Texans must have warped your mind. You know what I want. You."

Squeezing her eyes shut, she tried to stop the quaking that had started in her knees and had now spread to her hands. "Where are you?"

"Close. Real close, baby."

She breathed in a ragged, shallow breath and turned her back to Dee, who'd returned to the cookstove. "You're not to come near this ranch, Richard! Do you hear me?"

He laughed mockingly. "Or what? You'll sic some red-necked cowboy on me? The one you've been hanging around these past few days?"

Surely he didn't know Chance, she thought wildly. How could he? "No. I'll have you arrested."

His laughter grew harsh. "That's a good one, Lucinda. All I'll have to do is show them my Chicago badge and those hick town lawmen will be falling over their feet to make me feel welcome."

Rage shook her body. "I'm not coming back to you, Richard." She spoke through clenched teeth.

"Then you better warn those cowboy friends of yours to get ready for some fireworks. I've brought Sally with me. She's strapped right to my heart, and you know, Lucinda, I'm not a bit afraid to use her."

Lucinda very well knew that Sally was the name Richard had given his .38 revolver. She also knew that he wouldn't hesitate to kill with it if someone pushed him.

"You're sick!"

"I'm giving you until morning to leave that ranch, Lucinda, and come back to me."

"I'd rather die first!"

"You may just have to," he drawled softly, then clicked the phone dead.

Realizing he'd hung up on her, Lucinda placed the receiver back on its hook and took several deep breaths. It was nothing new for Richard to threaten to kill her, but it was something entirely different to draw Chance and his family into his demonic plans.

"Who was it, Lucy?"

Trying to collect herself as best she could, Lucinda went back to setting the table. Please God, she prayed, let her act normal. She couldn't let Dee suspect that anything was wrong.

"Actually, it was for me. My—friend in Chicago decided to call and wish me a Merry Christmas."

Dee carried a bowl of salad over to the table. "That's nice. But—" She frowned as she looked at Lucy fumbling with the cutlery. "Are you all right, Lucy? Your hands are shaking and you look pale!"

Lucinda forced herself to give Dee a reassuring smile. "Oh, I'm fine. I just heard some disturbing news, that's all. An old friend has been ill. But she's going to get better."

"That's good," she said patting Lucinda's shoulder. "I don't want you to be worried. Especially here at Christmastime."

Lucinda nodded, then turned away from Dee as a tidal wave of fear roiled through every fiber of her body.

Dear God, Richard had found her! What was she going to do? How was she going to protect Chance and his family now?

Chapter Eleven

Doctoring the bull turned out to be a bigger job than Chance had anticipated. By the time he and the other two hands got back to the ranch, it was well past dark and he was wet, cold and hungry. Most of all, he was eager to see Lucinda.

Chance hardly thought of himself as an authority on women. But he did know a woman's way of thinking was nothing like a man's. They usually acted on their feelings instead of logic. At least that's the way it was with the few women he'd know, including his mother and sister. So he could only believe that Lucinda wasn't any different. He believed her giving him the gift was more than just a Christmas gift. Just like he believed the passionate way she responded to him was more than just sexual. And tonight he intended to find out how she really felt about him.

"Have you and Lucy already eaten?" he asked a few minutes later as his mother placed a plate of warm food in front of him.

Dee took a seat at her son's elbow. "We gave up on you and ate about an hour ago."

He took up his fork and sliced into a cheese enchilada. "We would have been back earlier but that damn bull kicked down a panel and got away."

"I thought he was sick," Dee said.

"He is, but he decided he'd rather be sick than have us jabbing a needle of antibiotic into his neck."

"What did you do?"

A wry twist to his face, he said, "Chased him down with the Jeep."

"Oh? You were going to run him to good health?"

Dee poured him a cup of coffee and slid it over by his plate. Chance took a sip, then chuckled. "No. I got out on the front bumper and roped him. He jerked me off and dragged me for about twenty yards before he finally decided to give in and stop."

"Charles Delacroix! What possessed you to do such an idiotic thing? Why didn't you let go of the rope?"

He shook his head. "We were in the southeast pasture. It's so big that if he'd gotten completely away, we probably wouldn't have found him until the buzzards circled his carcass."

"Well, it's a miracle you weren't hurt," Dee scolded. "I told Lucy something unusual must have happened for you to be out so late in this weather."

He glanced around the quiet room and had to admit he was disappointed because Lucinda wasn't here sharing his supper and the day's happenings with him.

"Where is Lucy?"

"I think she went to her room. She said she was tired." Dee drummed her fingers against the tabletop. "Someone sent her flowers today."

Chance grimaced. "Yeah. She told me."

Dee studied her son's face. "It wasn't you?"

Frowning, he shook his head. "No. Damn it!"

"Well, there's no need for you to get hot about it. I just asked."

"I'm not hot about it," he muttered as he whacked off another bite of enchilada.

"Sarah Jane thinks Troy sent them," Dee went on.

A shaft of jealousy stabbed deep into Chance. "Troy has women falling all over him. He doesn't need to try to charm Lucy, too."

Dee's smile was thoughtful. "Troy will marry someday. But until then I don't think any young, beautiful woman like Lucinda is safe from him."

Like hell, Chance cursed inwardly. He loved his cousin, but he wasn't going to step aside and let him, or any man, have a clear path to Lucinda. She was meant for him. Each time he looked at her, touched her, his heart told him they belonged together. Not just until Christmas. But together for always. Somehow he had to convince her of that.

Two hours later, Lucinda was still shaking. Even though she kept telling herself that once she left in the morning, Chance and his family would be safe, she couldn't put the horror of hearing Richard's voice out of her mind.

Lucinda was thankful she'd worked so hard on the designs she'd made for Dee and Sarah Jane. They were all completed, except for a few details on Dee's dress. If she could ever get her hands to quit trembling, she could finish those tonight. In the morning, she'd be able to hand over the sketches, measurements, pattern pieces and fabric to Sarah Jane and feel confident that a good seamstress could complete the clothing.

She was attempting to mark a piece of pattern spread out over the bed when a knock sounded on the door. Before she could say to come in, Chance strode into the room.

Stepping away from the bed, Lucinda turned to face him. Immediately her gaze was drawn to the front of his jeans, which were caked with half-dried mud. His boots and the spurs she'd given him weren't in much better shape. But the sight of him was precious to her. So precious that tears stung the back of her eyes.

More than anything she longed to go to him, hold him close to her heart and pour out all her fears. But she couldn't take that risk. There was little doubt in her mind that if she didn't leave the ranch, Richard would carry out his threat. And she loved Chance too much to put his life in jeopardy.

"It looks like you've been in a wreck," she said.

"I was. With a bull."

Taking one step closer, she suddenly noticed a long scratch down the side of his face. "I hope you won."

One corner of his mouth lifted. "I did. This time."

He didn't say more and Lucinda wondered why he'd come to her room like this. To tempt her and make her more crazy than she already was?

"Did you—want to tell me something?"

Only about a thousand things, Chance thought as he closed the few small steps between them.

"I missed you at supper."

His words were like fingers clutching her heart. Glancing away from him, she said, "It was getting late and I had work to do."

She sounded so cool and aloof, nothing like the woman who'd squealed with pleasure at the sight of the newborn twin calves.

Raking his hand through the side of his hair, he said, "I know we talked today, Lucy. But I didn't get to say any of the things I wanted to say. That's why I'm here."

"Chance, if this is about last night," she said quickly, "I think it would be best if we forgot that completely."

His nostrils flared as he drew in a deep breath. "You mean forget that we nearly made love?"

She nodded, then finding it unbearable to keep looking up at his face, her gaze dropped to the toes of his boots. "We were—behaving recklessly, Chance."

"No. We were behaving naturally."

She looked up at him, her eyes questioning.

A brief smile touched his face. "Don't you think it's natural for a man and woman to be physically attracted to one another?"

"Yes, but—" Unable to explain the turmoil inside her, she turned away from him and went to stand next to the armchair by the window.

Chance stayed where he was and drank in the picture she made dressed in the same leggings and sweater he'd first found her in. But this time he didn't tell his eyes to stop their looking. Instead, he let them linger on her eyes and lips, her throat and breast, then on to the curvy line of her hips and legs. She was the most sensual woman he'd ever known and it turned him inside out just to look at her. But she was also much more. Like him, she was a survivor, a fighter, and he wanted her to be his wife, the mother of his children.

The certainty of his feelings compelled Chance to cross the room and place his hands upon her shoulders.

"You wanted me last night," he whispered. "Just as much as I wanted you."

The touch of his hands, the raw emotion on his face left a yearning so deep within Lucinda she wanted to weep.

"Yes, I did," she said, her voice solemn.

A light glinting in his gray eyes, he slid his hands up her throat, then cupped them both around her chin and jaws. "Then why are you saying we should forget it?"

Her heart banging against her ribs, she whispered, "Because it was just sex."

His face inched down toward hers until the curve of his lips was just a breath away from hers.

"You know that isn't true."

Her knees were beginning to feel like jelly and she wondered how much longer she could resist. If he didn't get out of here soon, she was afraid she was going to fall apart, tell him the truth about Richard's stalking and beg him to love her and keep her safe.

But Lucinda knew that Chance was the sort of man who would never back down from a fight. If she made him aware of Richard's threats, he'd make it a point to confront him. Chance was a strong, physical man, but that would hardly keep him safe from a psycho with a loaded revolver!

"I know that you're trying to seduce me," she murmured.

A grin parted his lips and exposed the edge of his teeth. The sight reminded Lucinda of how it had felt to have them nipping and tugging at her nipples, how it had felt to have a knot of desire burning inside of her.

"I'm trying to do that and a whole lot more," he said.

Drawing on every ounce of self-control she possessed, Lucinda brought her hands up against his chest and pushed him away. "I can't do this, Chance. I told you—"

He grabbed her hand and jerked her back to him. "You've told me a lot of things! None of which are the truth."

As she looked up at his grim face, everything inside Lucinda froze. "Like what?" she asked.

"Like you saying you didn't want a relationship with me or any man."

"That wasn't a lie," she shot back. "After what I've been through—" She stopped, horrified that she'd very nearly spilled the truth. "I don't want a man telling me when I can take a step, or eat. Or breathe. Or sleep!"

The vehemence of her words shocked him. "You think I'd be like that!"

No, she didn't really believe it. Chance would be a kind, passionate, loving man. She'd come to that realization some time ago. But it would be simpler to let him go on thinking otherwise.

"I don't know. I don't know you," she lied, her eyes carefully avoiding his.

"Then stay here and get to know me!"

Her eyes swung desperately back to his face. "I can't stay here and have an affair with you. Or whatever it is you want from me!"

Groaning with frustration, he shook his head. "You think I want you to have an affair? My God, Lucy, hasn't anything I've done or said registered with you?"

She swallowed in an attempt to free her throat of the painful knot choking her breath and stinging her eyes. "You don't understand, Chance. And I can't begin to explain—"

"No. *You* don't understand." Folding his hands around hers, he tugged her warm body up against his. "I'm asking you to marry me, Lucy. I want you to stay here on the ranch with me. Be my wife and the mother of my children."

She gasped softly as the impact of his words hit her. "Ma—marry you?"

His hands closed over her shoulders. "Lucy, I know you want to continue on with your career. And I know I'd be asking a lot of you to stay here, but—maybe you could ship your designs to sellers in the cities."

"You want to marry me?" she repeated in an awed whisper.

"Why are you so surprised? I've been trying to tell you—show you how I felt."

Dazed, Lucinda shook her head. "But after everything you told me about Jolene, I thought you never wanted to marry again."

"A week ago I would have cursed a blue streak if someone had told me I'd marry again. But you've changed me, Lucy. You've changed everything."

So had he, Lucinda thought desperately. A week ago, she'd had nothing on her mind but getting away from Richard's threats and starting up her career on the West Coast. She was still plagued with Richard's harassment, but everything else in her life had changed. For a short time, she'd seen what it was like to live within a family. She'd seen what it could be like to have a man really love her. Not possess her. As for her career, compared to her love for Chance, it was inconsequential.

"I—I'm glad that you feel differently now," she said as a lead weight began to fill her heart. "You're a wonderful man. You deserve to be happy."

His eyes delved gently into hers. "If you want me to be happy all you have to do is say yes."

With an anguished groan, she turned her back to him and bit down hard on her lip to keep from crying. "I—can't do that. I can't marry you, Chance."

Chance closed his eyes and told himself to be calm and patient. "Why? You don't want to be my wife? Are you afraid that if you become pregnant with my child, you'll die like Jolene did?"

Sick that he should think such a thing, Lucinda whirled back around to face him. "No! I don't think that at all!"

He shrugged. "I wouldn't blame you if you did. I believed that very thing for years."

"Well, I don't! Jolene's death was never your fault. I want you always to remember that."

Groaning, Chance drew her to him, pressed his cheek against hers. For a moment, Lucinda gave in to the pleasure of touching him, of filling her head with the scent of him. Soon the memories of these moments would be all she had. It wasn't fair. But then she'd learned years ago that life rarely was.

"I don't understand then, Lucy. Why can't you marry me?"

Why did he keep questioning her? she wondered miserably. Why was he going to force her to lie to him, to say something that would break her heart into a thousand tiny pieces?

Knowing she had no other choice, she pushed herself away from him and stared with burning eyes out the window. She'd been right when she'd told Chance that Santa never visited her, she thought. And obviously this year wouldn't be any different.

"I can't marry you, Chance, because I—I don't love you."

Chance felt as if someone had whacked him in the heart with an ax. He'd come to Lucy tonight eager to tell her how he felt about her and sharing the rest of his life with her. But now he was sick and angry for ever believing the two of them could have a future together as man and wife.

"Well, I—" A self-mocking laugh took over his words. "I didn't lie when I said I wasn't used to being around a woman. I guess I let my imagination run away with me. I thought last night was—it wasn't an act."

"It wasn't an act!" she whispered fiercely as pain began to seep through every inch of her body.

"I thought your gift today meant more than just a thank-you," he went on, his voice angry and accusing.

"It did mean more!" Dear God, he would never know how much more, she thought sickly. He would never know how much she wanted to fling herself in his arms, cry out how much she really adored him and how much she wanted to give him children, to love him for the rest of her life.

"If that's true, then no amount of time would be enough to figure you out. I sure as hell don't understand you, Lucy!"

Clenching her hands together to keep them from shaking out of control, she looked over her shoulder at him. "A woman can feel close to a man without loving him."

A cold, stoic look hardened his features. "Well, you've certainly proved that to me, Lucy. Besides showing me what an ignorant fool I am!"

"Chance—"

Before she could say more, he turned and strode angrily toward the door. Lucinda hurried after him and managed to grab his arm before he turned the knob to open it.

"Chance, you're not a fool!"

His head turned back to her and Lucinda suddenly realized she'd never really known what it was like to love someone until now. The pain she saw in his eyes was tearing into her, wounding her so deeply that she knew she would never heal.

"Then what am I, Lucy? What am I to you?"

She couldn't stop the rain of tears that began to pour down her face. "A wonderful man," she whispered hoarsely. "Always remember that."

With a muffled oath, he jerked her to him and kissed her with desperate, furious passion. Then suddenly he was out the door and slamming it behind him.

Lucinda fell against it, sobbing and shaking and wondering how she would ever survive to see tomorrow.

The next morning after breakfast, Lucinda went down to the horse stables to fetch Caesar. No matter what Chance thought of her now, she still wanted the kitten he'd given her.

Once she'd settled the animal into a cardboard box that he could travel comfortably in, she loaded it onto the front seat of her car, then went back into the house for her suitcases.

Her movements were stiff and automatic, her eyes dry and achy as Dee and Sarah Jane followed her outside to the waiting car.

"Lucy, this is crazy!" Dee exclaimed as Lucinda pushed the cases into the small back seat. "You'd already planned to stay for Christmas."

Lucinda slammed the door shut, then turned to face her friends. "I thought about that, Dee, and I've decided that it will be better if I leave now. Christmas is a time for family and I don't want to intrude on yours."

Looking around, Dee was relieved to see Chance approaching the three of them. "Thank God, you've shown up! Tell her not to leave, Chance. Tell Lucy that she *is* a part of this family."

He glanced at Lucinda and the look in his eyes dared her to admit to his mother why she was really leaving. If the whole thing hadn't been so horrendous, Lucinda could have laughed. Neither Chance nor Dee, would ever know the real reason she was leaving. They would never know how much she loved them all, how much she was willing to sacrifice, everything she'd ever wanted or dreamed of having in life, just so they would remain safe. And it was the right thing to do. That was the only thing holding Lucinda together now.

"Lucy knows what's best for her, Mother. And we have to respect that."

Dee stared incredulously at her son while Sarah Jane went to Lucinda and put her arms around her. "Lucy, we all love you and want you to be with us to celebrate. And to help us cook," she added jokingly.

"That's right," Dee spoke up. "Turkey and dressing. Pheasant and pumpkin pies. Lord, we'll never get it all done if you don't stay and help."

A quivering smile touched Lucinda's lips. "I'm betting you will. And I'll think about you. All of you," she added, her eyes going to Chance, "on Christmas Day."

His expression remained as stiff as it had been when she'd first looked at him this morning over the breakfast table. Unable to bear it any longer, Lucinda turned and climbed into the car.

"Goodbye now. And thank you for everything."

"Write to us," Dee called as the car engine sprang to life. "We'll send you pictures of the wedding."

Lucinda nodded and waved, then pressed down hard on the accelerator. She couldn't let them see that she was breaking apart.

It's all for the best, Lucy, she fiercely told herself as she guided the car away from the D Bar D. Once she left Texas behind, Chance and his family would be safe. And maybe, if she was lucky, she could dodge Richard long enough to make it across New Mexico. She'd take it one state at a time until she made it to California.

Once she got there, Lucinda was going to carefully change her looks and try to lose herself in the masses of San Diego. But then what? What was she going to do? How was she ever going to forget Chance and the love he'd offered her?

By the time she reached the end of the lane, Lucinda's eyes were so blurred with tears she was forced to pull to the side of the road and stop. With her forehead resting against the steering wheel, she sobbed so violently that her shoulders shook, tears drenched her face and soaked into the neck of her sweater.

She was so lost in her misery that she didn't hear another car pull up beside her, or the click of the driver's door as it swung open.

"Lucinda, this is all wrong. You sitting here crying, wasn't what I had planned, at all."

Icy fear shot through Lucinda as her head whipped around and she looked straight into the face of her darkest nightmares.

"Richard!"

A snarl on his face, he grabbed her arm and began jerking her out of the car. "It's high time you learned where you belong, little woman."

Chance had hoped that once Lucinda drove out of sight he could put her from his mind. But it wasn't working that way. He'd never felt so empty and lost in his life and the sad looks on the faces of his mother and sister weren't helping at all.

"I can't understand it," Dee said as she piled dirty dishes into the sink. "I was sure Lucy was enjoying herself here on the ranch. Then suddenly this morning she up and says she has to go."

Chance took a bite of a blueberry muffin, but it lodged in his throat like a wad of cotton. Cursing, he threw the rest of it into the trash and went to pour himself a cup of coffee. The hired hands were waiting on him down at the barn. They were going to have to doctor that damn bull again today, but at the moment Chance couldn't bring himself to go back outside and behave as though nothing were wrong.

Lucinda's leaving was all wrong. And he'd never be normal again.

"I feel like I've lost my sister," Sarah Jane said glumly as she plopped down at the breakfast counter. "Do you think she'll write to us?"

"I think so," Dee answered. "She'll surely want to know how the clothes for your honeymoon turned out. By the way," she added, "Lucy left the fabric and everything in a box in your room."

"I'll take it to Margie after Christmas," she told her mother, then with a thoughtful frown, she asked, "I wonder if Lucy remembered to take her flowers with her?"

Dee began to scrub the dirty breakfast plates. "I don't know. But her getting those flowers out of the blue like that still seems a bit odd to me."

There were a lot of things that seemed odd to Chance, he thought, as he carried his coffee over to the plate glass door and stared absently down at the barns.

Lucinda had said she didn't love him, but the look on her face and the tears in her eyes had spoken just the opposite. She'd said she hadn't been acting that night they'd come close to making love. She'd admitted the spurs were more than just a thank-you. What had she really been trying to say to him? That she loved him but was just afraid to admit it? But why? he wondered as frustration clawed at his insides. Why should she be afraid to love him? She'd said he was a wonderful man. To always remember that.

Suddenly, like the flashing frames of a movie, Chance's mind was filled with scenes of Lucinda. Her first night here and how frantic and desperate she'd been to get back on the road, the terror on her face when she'd first seen Troy and his patrol car. She was afraid of policemen, she'd told him. Because Richard had been a policeman. When Chance broke all that down, he realized she'd simply been saying she was afraid of her ex-fiancé.

"Damn!"

Dee turned around to see Chance slamming his coffee cup down on the dining table. "Where are you going?" she asked as he started out of the kitchen.

Ignoring his mother's question, Chance hurried to Lucinda's bedroom. He found it neat and everything in its place. She hadn't left a thing behind that might give him a hint as to where she was headed. Even the Christmas bouquet he'd seen last night on her dresser was gone now. Or was it?

Jerking up the small wastebasket beside the bed, he found the red flowers shredded to tiny bits. Even the little stuffed bear had been torn into several pieces and tossed in with the rest as though it were all nasty garbage.

This wasn't like Lucinda at all. She was a woman who loved beauty in any sort of form. She wouldn't deliberately destroy a gift. No, this was an act of helpless desperation.

"Mother! Mother!"

Hearing the urgency in her son's voice, Dee raced down the hallway and met her son coming out of Lucinda's bedroom. "What is it? What's wrong?"

"Did anything strange or different happen to Lucinda yesterday? Or last night?"

Not sure how her son's mind was working, Dee looked at him blankly. "Something strange? What do you mean? Why?"

He let out an impatient breath and took his mother gently by the shoulders. "Did she get a letter, or a phone call? Anything?"

"She got flowers. But you knew that," she said, then her brows puckered together as something else registered. "Now that you mention it, she did get a phone call right before supper. She said it was a friend from Chicago.''

"Did she say anything else? Please, Mother, think! It's important!''

"Well, all that I remember is that she was pretty shaken after she'd hung up the phone. She said something about it being bad news but that everything was going to be all right.''

"That's it!''

Spinning away from his mother, Chance jogged toward the front door. "Call Troy and tell him to head toward the ranch. If he sees Lucy along the way, stop her!''

Stunned, Dee stared at him. "Stop her? But Chance—''

"Just do it! I'll explain later,'' he shouted, already halfway down the steps.

Right now he had to find Lucinda, he thought desperately, as he raced toward his truck. He had to find her before she drove into danger. Before Chance lost her forever!

Chapter Twelve

The moment Richard attempted to shove Lucinda into his car, she went at him kicking and clawing for all she was worth. Cursing a stream of threats at her, he wrenched her arm behind her back and bent her head towards the open door.

Knowing she'd never escape if he got her inside the vehicle, Lucinda called on every bit of strength she had in her and slammed her knee into his groin.

The unexpected pain caused his grip to loosen just enough for Lucinda to wrench herself away from him. Her breaths coming fast and labored, she raced down the muddy graveled road in the direction of the ranch.

Before she had traveled twenty yards, Richard caught up to her and tripped her from behind. She fell face forward, her hands and belly grinding into the rocks and mud and gravel.

When Chance drove up on the scene, Richard was jerking her up by the arm and a handful of hair at the back of her head.

Wild with fear, he stomped on the brakes, sending the pickup into a sideways skid. It had barely come to a stop in the middle of the road before he jumped out and ran toward Lucinda and her attacker.

"Let go of her, you bastard!"

With a death grip on Lucinda's arm, the crazed man reached into his coat and drew out a revolver.

Lucinda screamed as he pointed the .38 at Chance.

"No! Get back, Chance! He's crazy, he'll kill you!"

"You better listen to her, cowboy. I'd sooner shoot you than her. But if I have to, I'll kill you both."

"You're not going to shoot anybody," Chance growled. His face dark with rage, he continued walking toward Lucinda and her captor. "You're going to let Lucy go and then you're going to throw down that gun."

Richard cocked the pistol and began to laugh. "Like hell!"

Sobbing now, Lucinda looked frantically around her, searching for anything to divert Richard's attention. Like a miracle from heaven, she saw a sheriff's patrol car pulling off the highway and heading toward them.

"Here comes Troy!" she shouted.

Richard twisted his head to look at the approaching car. The moment he did, Chance pounced. Grabbing the arm holding the gun, he whammed it across his raised knee.

The blow knocked the gun loose from Richard's hand. Without the weapon, he was no match for Chance's physical strength. With a right fist in his eye, Richard staggered backward and released his grip on Lucinda. Another blow from Chance's left fist and Richard toppled into the ditch.

As he lay there groaning and helpless, Chance turned to Lucinda. Sobbing, she fell into his arms. He gathered her tightly against him, buried his face in the side of her neck and stroked his hand down the back of her hair.

"It's all right, Lucy. Don't cry, darling. Everything is going to be all right now."

"But Richard will get away! He'll come back and—"

"No! He'll never come back here, Lucy. He'll never hurt you again. I promise you that."

Troy pulled Richard from the ditch and handcuffed him. As the young sheriff prodded his prisoner back to the patrol car, Chance found the .38 where it had fallen and gave it to his cousin. Dazed and shivering, Lucinda clung to Chance's arm as the four of them headed to the patrol car.

"He was threatening to kill us," Chance told Troy.

"I know. I saw the three of you when I drove up. Who is he anyway? Do you two know him?"

Lucinda nodded and spoke as best she could through chattering teeth. "He's Richard Winthrop from Chicago. And he's been stalking me for the past several months."

"You don't have anything on me," Richard snarled. "I never stalked this woman! She's lying!"

"Sure, buddy," Troy said, "that's why you were trying to kill her."

"I'm warning you, I'm a homicide detective on the Chicago police force," he threatened the sheriff. "I'll have your head for this!"

Troy shoved him into the patrol car. "Well, Mr. Homicide Detective, you did the wrong thing when you came to Parmer County. I can assure you of that. I'm gonna see that you're put away for a long time."

He slammed the door shut, then turned back to Chance and Lucinda. "Are you two going to be okay?"

Chance nodded soberly as his arm came around Lucinda's shoulders. "We are now. Do we need to come in and give statements?"

"You can do that later," Troy said, seeing the way Lucinda was still shaking and clinging to his cousin. "When Lucy feels up to it will be soon enough."

As Troy drove away, Chance gently led Lucinda back to his pickup. Once they were inside on the bench seat, he didn't say anything, he simply wrapped his jacket around her and held her tightly to him.

Finally, after several minutes had passed and the quaking of her body began to subside, she said, "I'm so sorry, Chance. So very sorry."

Pressing his cheek against the top of her head, he asked, "What is there for you to be sorry about?"

She brought her head up to look at him, her eyes begging him for forgiveness. "I nearly got you killed! Last night Richard called and—he threatened to kill you and your family if I didn't leave! I should have never stayed at your ranch. I led him here and he almost—"

"Shh! Don't do this, Lucy. Don't blame yourself for anything. The man is obviously deranged."

Shaking her head, she cupped her hands around the sides of his face. "You know why I had to leave you now, don't you? You know why I couldn't accept your proposal?"

He shook his head with regret. "I know you were afraid. What I don't understand is why you didn't confide in me. I love you, Lucy. Don't you know I'd fight any demon for you?"

Tears began to roll down her face. After the heartache of leaving Chance this morning and then experiencing the wild fear that he was going to be killed in front of her very eyes, she couldn't believe that he was really holding her, telling her that he loved her.

"That's what I was afraid of. I knew if I told you about Richard, you'd go after him. And I knew he carried a gun and I didn't want you to put yourself in that kind of danger. I'd rather he killed me first than for you to be hurt."

Lucinda shuddered as she relived the fear that had paralyzed her when she'd looked up to see Richard standing outside her car door. "I've been afraid for a long time now, Chance. For months and months I've lived in fear. I tried getting protection from the police, but that turned out to be a joke. Richard *was* the police. I couldn't get any help there, and since I had no family, my last hope was to leave Chicago and find a new place to make my home."

"You found it, Lucy. With me. Are you still going to say that you don't love me?"

She wiped at the tears that continued to streak down her face. "Forgive me for lying to you, Chance. But I did it because I do love you. More than my life."

He lifted her palm to his lips, then grimaced as his lips tasted the salty blood of her scraped and cut skin. He knew it would be a long, long time before he'd be able to forget the image of Lucinda being manhandled by that maniac, the sight of her helpless and weeping and begging Chance to save himself rather than try to help her.

"You just proved that to me, Lucy. Now if you'll say you're going to marry me, I'll forgive you anything."

He smiled at her, and the warm, loving light in his eyes made all the terror of the past few minutes fade away like a bad dream.

"Then forgive me," she whispered. "Because I am going to marry you. I'm going to give you children. And I'm going to love you with all my heart for the rest of our lives."

His sigh was full of elation and contentment as he leaned his head toward hers and gently kissed her lips. "Then living on a ranch with a cowboy isn't going to be a problem for you? I know your career is—"

With a shake of her head, she quickly pressed her lips back to his and kissed him with all the fervor of her love. "My career will be just fine," she murmured against his cheek. "I'll find some way to get my designs on the market. In fact, your sister had a great idea about that. But you and our children will always come first in my life. Just remember that."

"Well, one thing is for sure, Lucy," he said, rubbing his nose against hers. "You'll never have to be afraid of anything or anyone again. I'll always be around to rescue you if you need it."

At this moment he couldn't have said anything that would have made her feel more safe and secure and loved. Her heart was fairly bursting with it as she smiled and sighed with utter contentment.

"If you'll go get Caesar, I'll be ready to go home," she told him, then in afterthought, she asked, "What about my car?"

"I'll send a couple of the hands for it," Chance assured her.

He went after the kitten, who was still safely ensconced in his box on the front seat of Lucinda's car.

Once Chance was back at the pickup and had settled the animal in the crook of Lucinda's arm, he started the engine, then winked at her and grinned. "You know what tonight is. It's Christmas Eve. And on Christmas Eve, Santa always comes to the Delacroix's house."

"Does he really?" Lucinda asked as she did her best to look skeptical.

"I promise."

Her expression suddenly turned very provocative. "I believe you."

"You do?" he asked, his brows lifted with surprise.

Her face wreathed with joy, she laughed. "Well, he is going to give me a cowboy for Christmas, isn't he?"

Chance's eyes were bright, shining with the love he promised to give her tonight and always.

"He is," he said with certainty. Then leaning over, he murmured against her lips, "Merry Christmas, darling."

A month later, Lucinda was in the kitchen trying her hand at making piecrust when her husband came in carrying the mail.

Stomping the snow off his boots, he tossed a stack of letters onto the breakfast counter, then carried a single envelope over to Lucinda. "You know," he said, glancing around the kitchen. "It's still hard to believe we have the house to ourselves. With Mother and Doc leaving for their honeymoon yesterday and Sarah Jane gone on a skiing trip with her friends, we won't know what to do with ourselves."

Lucinda slanted her husband a provocative look. "Oh, I'm sure you'll think of something."

Chuckling softly, he grinned sexily at her. "I'll try my best. But I'll let you read your letter first."

Before Lucinda took the envelope from him, she kissed him, then handed him a cup of hot coffee.

"Oh, it's from Molly," Lucinda said as she glanced at the return address.

"Open it and see what she has to say," Chance urged.

Lucinda ripped open the envelope. Inside it there was a short note with a newspaper clipping attached to it.

Dear Lucy, I was so happy to hear about your marriage and the happy life you've found out there in Texas.

I found this clipping in the newspaper yesterday and thought you might like to read it. Take care and I promise to write more next time.

Love, your friend, Molly

Smiling, Lucinda turned her attention to the scrap of newspaper. It was small, but as far as Lucinda was concerned, the significance of what it said couldn't be measured.

"What is it, honey?" Chance asked as he watched a myriad of emotions cross his wife's face.

Smiling as though a thousand angels had suddenly descended on the kitchen, she handed the piece of paper to Chance.

"It's about Richard. Molly found it in a Chicago newspaper. I'm glad that his friends and fellow policemen up there finally know that he's serving time in a Texas jail and is undergoing psychiatric therapy. And not only that, after some internal investigations back in Chicago, the state has found Richard guilty of taking bribes from criminals. So after his jail time is up here in Texas, he'll be locked up in Illinois for a long time to come."

Chance shook his head with disbelief. "Too bad it couldn't have happened sooner. When you needed their help, they all believed Richard and pegged you for a scorned woman out for revenge because of your broken engagement. I can't begin to imagine the terror you must have lived through back then."

Yes, her life had once been one long nightmare. But now, surrounded by Chance's love, she was putting it all behind her. "It was like being condemned to hell with no way out. But thank God, that's all in the past now and Richard has been put away where he can't harm anyone else. And he'll be there for many long years."

"The man got exactly what he deserved," Chance said with conviction.

Lucinda tossed the clipping into a nearby trash basket, then curling her arms around her husband's neck, she whispered, "And we got just what we deserved, too, my darling. We got each other."

* * . * * *

MILLION DOLLAR SWEEPSTAKES (III)

The Loop™

Is the future what it's cracked up to be?

This December, discover what commitment
is all about in

GETTING ATTACHED: CJ
by Wendy Corsi Staub

C. J. Clarke was tired of lugging her toothbrush
around town, and she sure didn't believe longtime
boyfriend David Griffin's constant whining about
"not being able to commit." He was with her every
day—and most nights—so what was his problem?
C.J. knew marriage wasn't always what it was cracked
up to be, but when you're in love you're supposed to
end up happily ever after...aren't you?

The ups and downs of life as you know it continue with

GETTING A LIFE: MARISSA
by Kathryn Jensen (January)

GETTING OUT: EMILY
by ArLynn Presser (February)

Get smart. Get into "The Loop"!

Only from

Silhouette®

where passion lives.

LOOP5

HE'S MORE THAN A MAN,
HE'S ONE OF OUR

IDEAL DAD
Elizabeth August

Eight-year-old Jeremy Galvin knew Murdock Parnell would make the perfect dad. Now it was up to Murdock to persuade Jeremy's mom, Irene, that he was the ideal husband for her.

Ideal Dad, available in January, is the third book in Elizabeth August's bestselling series, WHERE THE HEART IS.

Look for *Ideal Dad* by Elizabeth August—available in January.

Fall in love with our Fabulous Fathers!

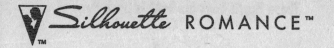

Silhouette ROMANCE™

BELIEVING IN MIRACLES
by
Linda Varner

Carpenter Andy Fulbright and Honorine "Honey" Truman had all the criteria for a perfect marriage—they liked and respected each other, they desired and needed each other...and *neither* one loved the other! But with the help of some mistletoe and two young elves, these two might learn to believe in the miracle of Christmas....

BELIEVING IN MIRACLES is the second book in Linda Varner's MR. RIGHT, INC., a heartwarming series about three hardworking bachelors in the building trade who find love at first sight— construction site, that is!

Don't miss BELIEVING IN MIRACLES, available in December. And look for Book 3, WIFE MOST UNLIKELY, in March 1995. Read along as old friends make the difficult transition to lovers....

Only from **Silhouette®**

where passion lives.

Those Harris boys are back in book three of...

by Sandra Steffen

Three sexy, single brothers bet they'll never say "I do."
But the Harris boys are about to discover their vows of bachelor-
hood don't stand a chance against the forces of love!

You met Mitch in BACHELOR DADDY #1028 (8/94) and Kyle in
BACHELOR AT THE WEDDING #1045 (11/94). Now it's time for
brother Taylor to take the marriage plunge in—

EXPECTANT BACHELOR #1056 (1/95): When Gina Jenson sets
out to seduce the handsome Taylor, he's in for the surprise of his
life. Because Gina wants him to father her child!